THE Great BRAIN ROBBERY

THE *Great* BRAIN ROBBERY

ANNA KEMP

SIMON AND SCHUSTER

First published in Great Britain in 2013 by Simon and Schuster UK Ltd
A CBS COMPANY

1 3 5 7 9 10 8 6 4 2

Simon & Schuster UK Ltd
1st Floor,
222 Gray's Inn Road
London
WC1X 8HB

Simon & Schuster Australia, Sydney
Simon & Schuster India, New Delhi

A CIP catalogue record for this book is available from the British Library.

ISBN 978-0-85707-996-1

Printed and bound by CPI Group (UK) Ltd, Croydon, CR0 4YY

For

my brainy and beloved husband Jim

CHAPTER ONE
The Mechanimals

What is the best question ever? Answer: What do you want for your birthday? Well now, let me see. I would like a train-set, and a mermaid outfit, and one of those time-machines that sends you back to the days when there was no school and people had dinosaurs for pets – pleeeeeease!

I love presents. I bet you do too. Problem is, you don't always get what you asked for. And that's because some things are just 'too many pennies', as my nan used to say. Frankie Blewitt did not have many pennies, so he did not have many toys. But, all the same, there was one toy that Frankie really, really wanted. One toy that would make all his dreams come true. It was the toy of toys. The toy to end all toys. The Greatest Toy of All. It was, of course, a *Mechanimal.* What do you mean, 'What's a *Mechanimal*?'? Wake up! Pay attention! For those of you who have been living on the moon, Mechanimals are the most wanted toys on the planet Earth: Gadget the Rabbit! Sparky the Squirrel! Gigawatt the Gila Monster! In shiny blue, or sparkly pink, or glow-in-the-dark green. And Gadget the Rabbit was right at the top of Frankie's birthday wishlist – double underlined and surrounded by stick-on stars. But Frankie knew he was never going to get one. So as soon as he had finished his list, he tore it up and threw it in the bin.

Not having a Mechanimal was a big problem

for Frankie. Not because he was a greedy little so-and-so, but because he was the only kid in school who didn't have one. Every lunchtime Frankie's classmates would grab their Mechanimals from their rucksacks, run to the playground and play Mechanimal Farm or Battle Mechanimal. But Frankie just had to watch. None of this would have been so bad if Frankie's friends had been around, but his best friend Neet was off school with chickenpox, and his pal Wes had moved away. So every lunchtime, Frankie sat on a bench at the edge of the playground, stared at his trainers, and waited for Mrs Pinkerton to blow the whistle – which wasn't much fun at all.

But Frankie's problems didn't end there. They were made a whole lot worse by a new arrival: Timothy Snodgrass. Little Timmy Snodgrass was one of those children who got everything on his wishlist and some extras besides. All he had to do was blink his big blue eyes and say, 'But Mummy, Mummy! A Mechanimal spaceship is the only thing I have ever really wanted!' and, before you knew it, he not only had a spaceship but a funhouse, farm and fairground too. As you can imagine, having all those toys made Timmy an instant hit with his classmates. When the schoolbell rang at the end of the day, everyone would race over to Timmy's to play in his spectacular playroom – everyone, that is, except Frankie. No Mechanimal meant no invitation to Timmy's. So Frankie would pack up his schoolbag and set off home alone. It was the worst feeling ever. Or so Frankie thought. Then, one drizzly September afternoon, things got even worse.

It was the end of the school day and everyone was whispering excitedly about Timmy's new Mechanimal racetrack. Frankie didn't expect to be invited, so he collected his things and tried to slink away before anybody noticed. But it was too late. As he headed for the door, a pair of smart new trainers stepped into his path.

'Aren't you coming round to play?'

Frankie looked up in surprise. Timmy was standing in front of him smiling. The sort of smile you'd see on a venomous snake.

'Oh, sorry,' Timmy smirked. 'I forgot. You don't have a Mechanimal, do you? What dreadful luck. Oh well, I guess you'll just have to go home and play with the beetles under your bed.'

The whole class went silent. Frankie could feel their eyes on his skin and his face began to prickle. He moved to walk out of the door but Timmy blocked him again.

'I bet they all have names, don't they? Your beetle friends.'

The class giggled nervously. They didn't want to annoy Timmy. He had a Mechanimal racetrack after all. Frankie felt a tightening in his throat. He tried to think of something clever to say but his mind was buzzing like a TV screen when it goes all black and white and blizzardy. He screwed up his eyes to try and shut the buzzing out but it just grew louder and louder until suddenly he blurted:

'SHUT UP, Timmy! I actually HAVE a Mechanimal! I just don't want to play with YOU, because you're a—' Then Frankie said a very rude word that I mustn't repeat.

Timmy's face went pink and his eyes turned into thin little slots, making his head look rather like a piggy bank. 'Oh, really,' he snorted. 'Well we'll see about that.' Timmy lunged forward, seized Frankie's rucksack and tipped it upside-down. Books, pencils and bits of old sandwich went tumbling onto the mucky floor of the cloakroom along with a two-pound coin that started rolling quickly away.

'Hmmm . . . I don't see any Mechanimals here,' Timmy scoffed. The class was in fits of giggles, but Frankie wasn't listening. He had dived to the floor to stop the coin from rolling under the lockers. He had been given it to buy some bread for dinner and couldn't afford to lose it. Frankie's knees skidded across the rough carpet then *WALLOP!* he collided heavily with a locker-door, knocking a deep dent in its side. The class howled with laughter.

'What's all this fuss?! Shhh! Quiet children!' Mrs Pinkerton came bustling through the crowd like a pink rhinoceros and stopped in front of Frankie, her hands planted squarely on her enormous hips. 'Frankie Blewitt!' she honked. 'What on earth are you doing? Look at your knees! What a mess!'

'Frankie slipped over,' said the treacherous Timmy, blinking his big, blue eyes. 'It wasn't his fault, Miss.'

'Well it is very noble of you to stand up for your friend, Timmy,' cooed Mrs Pinkerton, patting his curly head, 'but I know trouble when I see it. Now pick up your things, Frankie, and go home!'

'But I—'

'NOW, Frankie!'

Frankie couldn't believe the total unfairness of it all. It was SO unfair – even more unfair than the time he had got blamed for teaching the class budgie to say 'Mrs *Stink*erton' – which he hadn't! (Though right now he sort of wished he had.) Frankie looked around at the faces staring down at him. Timmy was standing behind the teacher mouthing something silently: *Frankie – no – friends.* Frankie felt his ears burn with embarrassment, but before he had the chance to say anything, the whole class snatched up their coats and, without a glance in his direction, hurtled off to Timmy's house, sprinting and jumping and shrieking like fireworks.

Frankie felt like a punctured balloon. He picked himself up and slowly dragged himself home. His knees were raw in the chilly September air and his cheeks stung with tears as he tried to rub them away with the itchy cuff of his school jumper.

'Urrrrgh . . . stupid . . . Timmy . . .' he muttered angrily. 'Stupid . . . stupid . . . urrrrrgh!' Frankie didn't want anyone at home to see his red eyes, so he took the long route to let them cool off a bit. He always took the long route when he'd had a bad day. That was because it took him past the doors of the most marvellous, the most extraordinary, the most spectacular toyshop in the world: Marvella Brand's Happyland.

CHAPTER TWO
MARVELLA'S

Marvella's was a new addition to the village of Cramley-on-the-Crump. When the news broke that a Marvella's was opening the local children gasped with joy. And when they heard that this Marvella's would be the biggest in the country, the children gasped so deeply they almost turned themselves inside-out. You see, Marvella Brand's Happyland was more than your regular toy emporium. It was an enchanted kingdom, a magical realm where all your dreams came true – dreams you hadn't even had yet,

MARVELLA BRAND'S

dreams of things you didn't even know were possible.

Frankie stopped on the pavement outside the shop and gazed up at this magical dream castle. Brightly-coloured flags flew from masts, turrets sparkled like candied fruit, and two red-cheeked toy soldiers stood guard at the entrance. Above the door, 'Marvella's' was spelt out in glittering letters and, perched on top of these was the store's famous mascot, Teddy Manywishes, waving and smiling mechanically. The shop wasn't yet open so the golden doors were still tightly shut. But peering through the window, Frankie could see boxes being stacked on the shelves in preparation for the grand opening. Pride of place, of course, went to the store's star toys: the Mechanimals. Row upon gleaming row of them, like a miniature army, and leading the charge was Frankie's favourite – a smart blue Gadget the Rabbit.

Now you've probably been wondering what's so special about Mechanimals. Well let me tell you. A Mechanimal is not just any robotic pet. It is much much more. Each and every Mechanimal is specially programmed to recognise you, its owner. From the moment it sets its electronic eyes on your beaming face, your Mechanimal becomes your most devoted friend. It doesn't tease you, or ignore you, or sulk when you don't share your crisps. It doesn't tip your schoolbag out on the floor or snitch to the teacher. No, your Mechanimal thinks you are the best thing since stripy pyjamas. It will follow you to the ends of the earth and love you for as long as its batteries last – guaranteed.

Frankie pressed his head against the cold glass of the window and sighed. He really needed a friend. Even a mechanical one would have done just fine.

With all the teasing and trouble and grazing

of knees, Frankie had almost forgotten that the next day was his tenth birthday. He closed his eyes and imagined how brilliant it would be to come downstairs and see a Gadget-the-Rabbit-shaped present on the kitchen table. But he knew it was impossible. Marvella Brand's Happyland could make all your dreams come true, but not if you were skint. Frankie pushed his nose down into his scarf and trudged slowly home.

Frankie Blewitt hadn't always been skint. In fact, his parents, Mr and Mrs Blewitt, had been jolly well-off indeed. So well-off in fact that Frankie used to slurp his choco pops from a solid silver spoon. But if you know Frankie as well as I do, then you will know that, the year before, Mr and Mrs Blewitt got mixed up in some rather dodgy business that landed them both in jail. Frankie hadn't heard from them since. Not a word. Not so much as a Christmas card. Mr and Mrs Blewitt were not exactly the nicest of parents and, as far as I'm concerned, they can stay in prison for a while longer. But with his parents gone, Frankie's pocket money soon dried up. Mr Blewitt had taken care to stash his millions in far-flung places and Frankie did not receive a bean. Luckily for him, his old French nanny, Alphonsine, took him under her wing and Frankie had lived with her, her husband Eddie and their fluffy French poodle Colette ever since.

Alphonsine and Eddie did not have a penny-chew between them. But being broke didn't bother them much. After all they had seen worse – much worse – during the war many years ago.

'Pffff!' Alphonsine would splutter as she whisked her pancake mixture. 'Do not worry about such things, little cabbage. There is worse things in life than not having the newest wotsit on the telly-box. Pffffff!' Indeed, Alphonsine did not see the point in *buying* new wotsits when she could make them herself. She had spent most of the war working as a secret agent in the French Resistance and had spent much of that time sabotaging tanks and fixing bicycles. As a result she was an extremely skilled mechanic who could do pretty much anything with her spanner. If Eddie, Frankie or Colette ever needed something, Alphonsine would jump on her motorbike and head down to the local dump. There, she would scavenge for bits and bobs – a bolt here, a nut there – and *hey presto*! New kettle! New armchair! New bike for Frankie! But Alphonsine wouldn't just fix things. No. She would improve them by adding special features of her own. So the kettle whistled the French national anthem when the water boiled and Frankie's bike blew out lovely big bubbles when he turned the pedals.

Frankie loved Alphonsine and Eddie and by the time dinner was on the table his tears had dried and he was already feeling much better. Then, as they were eating, a news report on the soon-to-be-open Marvella store flashed up on the telly.

'Look!' said Frankie. 'There's going to be a new Marvella's, just down the road. How great is that!' Eddie removed his spectacles and blinked his misty eyes.

'Do you see this, Alphonsine?' he asked, turning up the volume. Alphonsine craned her wrinkly old neck towards the television.

'A Marvella's?' she said. 'In Cramley-on-ze-Crump?' Eddie nodded and Alphonsine raised her bristly white eyebrows. Frankie couldn't work out why they were acting so strangely.

'What?' he asked. 'Do you know something I don't?'

'Marvella's has a long and curious history, you know,' added Eddie.

'Really?' said Frankie, intrigued.

'Oh, yes,' said Alphonsine. 'It all started many yonks ago when we were just tiny tiddlers. Tell him ze story, Eddie.' Eddie turned off the TV and began.

Chapter Three
The Smile

'When I was a small boy, there was a gentleman in the next village called Mr Crispin Whittle.' Eddie spoke with the same precision and care that he used to spoon sugar into his tea. 'Mr Whittle was a carpenter. He earned his living making door frames, crates and tables. But Mr Whittle found all that rather dull. So, once the day's work was over, he would gather together the leftover wood, take it to his workshop in the forest and sit up all night long crafting the most *exquisite* toys imaginable.' Eddie's eyes shone like polished buttons. 'Sometimes, my friends and I would go there late in the evening to see what he was making.'

'What sorts of toys did he make?' asked Frankie.

'Oh, the most fabulous things you can think of: splendid castles with moats full of mechanical fish; wind-up dragons that puffed out jets of green fire; painted clockwork unicorns big enough for small princesses to ride. At first he made gifts for his nieces and nephews, but Mr Whittle couldn't bear to see other children left out, so he was soon making gifts for everyone.'

'Did he make anything for you?' asked Frankie.

'But of course!' said Alphonsine. 'Show him, Eddie.' Eddie hobbled over to a dresser in the next room, rummaged around and came back holding what looked like a walnut. Frankie took it out of Eddie's hand and inspected it. It *was* a walnut.

‘Open it,’ prompted Eddie. Frankie saw that there was a small, golden clasp at the join of the shell. He nudged it gently with his fingernail and, as the nut popped open, a tinkling waltz began to play. Frankie looked closer and saw, carved into the inside of the shell, a dozen miniature mechanical dancers sweeping around a tiny, Viennese ballroom. He was completely spellbound.

‘But it was not always hunky-monkey for Mr Crispin,’ said Alphonsine, taking over the story. ‘It was not long before every king and queen in Europe was wanting Mr Whittler to make toys for their little princelings. But princelings, as you know, is generally rotten eggs.’

‘Do you mean spoiled rotten?’ asked Frankie, trying not to giggle.

‘Yes, yes,’ said Alphonsine impatiently, ‘spoiled eggrot. And the most rottenest egg of all was His Royal Highness the Prince of Valkrania.’

Eddie nodded and rolled his eyes in agreement. 'Well this royal princeling,' Alphonsine continued, 'wants to impress all his royal friends. So he orders his mother to get him a pair of wings, made of real feathers, so that he can swoop about the sky like an eagle. Now, Mr Whittler is a toymaker, but he is not a magician. The queen, she is saying, "*Do this*", "*Do that*", and "*I command you!*" But Mr Whittler tells her, "*You can command me all you like, Your Majesty, but I cannot change the laws of gravity.*"

'So Mr Whittler is working night after night, but no amount of cleverness will do the trick. The big day arrives and Prince Vladimir is given a most beauteous pair of eagle wings, but Mr Whittler tells him they is just for play. They is toys. The prince can flap about all he likes, he can even glide a bit, but he should not do anything knuckle-brained like jump out of his bedroom window, because gravity will get the better of him, no doubts about it! But of course the Royal Doughnut doesn't listen. He huffs and puffs and he says to himself, "*If I want to go jumping out of the window then I jolly well shall! Who does this gravity fellow think he is?*" And that very afternoon, he invites all his friends to the palace, jumps out of the royal window and breaks his royal schnozz.' Alphonsine demonstrated the prince's crash landing with her spoon as Frankie spluttered with laughter.

'Straight away,' Alphonsine went on, her eyes sparkling, 'everyone is saying that the prince is a butt.'

'Eh?' said Frankie, confused.

'Yes, yes,' said Alphonsine, 'he is the butt of all jokes, the stock of laughing.'

'A *laughing stock*, dear,' said Eddie.

'Zat is what I said,' puffed Alphonsine. 'He is

the laughing butt, the biggest laughing butt in all the kingdom!' Frankie chortled with delight. 'So he sends out his army to catch this rascally Mr Gravity, but of course Gravity is a most tricksy fellow to catch. So what does the great nincomboob y do but arrest poor Mr Whittler instead.'

'Oh, no,' said Frankie, 'what happened to him?'

'Ah,' said Eddie sadly, slipping the walnut into his jacket pocket. 'Mr Whittle was thrown in jail – and there he stayed until his poor old heart gave out.'

'That's awful,' said Frankie.

'Awful indeed,' said Eddie, 'but the story doesn't end there. When he passed away, Mr Whittle's workshop was inherited by his youngest and most beloved niece – a tiny girl of six called Marvella Brand.' Frankie pricked up his ears.

'Marvella was a little dear. She was always clutching a sparkling fairy wand that her uncle had crafted for her and she had a charming pink smile that never quite left her lips.'

'Except for once,' Alphonsine interrupted, slurping up a string of spaghetti. 'The day she is told of her dear uncle's death.'

'That's right,' said Eddie, his voice dropping to a whisper. 'They say that on hearing the news, little Marvella's smile instantly vanished and her eyes iced over like two wintry pools.' Frankie shuddered. 'From that moment on,' Eddie continued, 'Marvella's smile was never quite the same again. It came back, but it was more static, more stiff around the edges. And it never quite melted those two frozen eyes.'

'What happened to her?' Frankie asked.

'Well she turned her uncle's workshop into the booming business you see today,' said Eddie.

'Little Marvella became one of the richest tycoons in the world. But it is said that she has never recovered from the death of her uncle.'

'What do you mean?' said Frankie.

'Well,' Eddie continued, 'children may love Marvella Brand, but she certainly doesn't love them back. She blames them for what happened to her poor uncle, you see, and she has never, ever forgiven them.'

Frankie felt a chill on the back of his neck. Perhaps it was the draught. He wasn't sure.

'That is enough chatterboxing,' smiled Alphonsine, 'it is late and it is somebody's birthday tomorrow, is it not?'

Frankie grinned and yawned. It had been a long day and he was ready to put it behind him. He finished his dinner and clambered up the stairs to bed. But sleep did not come easily. Frankie tweaked back the curtains and watched a dark, starless sky swirling over the house like an enormous whirlpool. An electrical storm was brewing. He buried himself deep in his blankets and, as the thunder rolled overhead, he began to dream the strangest, most vivid dreams. In his mind's eye, he saw an army of Mechanimals marching out of Marvella's golden doors. Nobody could control their movements and nobody could switch them off. They just kept marching and marching and marching, row after row after row of them, on and on and on.

CHAPTER FOUR
THE FIGHT

When Frankie woke up, he couldn't believe it was the same bedroom he had gone to sleep in. The storm had cleared the air and a bright sunshine reached through the window and tickled him under the chin. But, best of all, it was his birthday! Frankie bounced out of bed as if he were made of springs and ran downstairs, to where Alphonsine and Eddie were waiting for him with big wrinkly smiles.

'HAAAAPEEEE BURRSSDAY FRANKIEEEEE!' sang Alphonsine. The breakfast table was laid and in the centre was a fresh pile of pancakes topped with ten birthday candles. Frankie glanced along the table but there was no sign of a present. He felt a sharp stab of disappointment, then blushed with shame. Alfie and Eddie couldn't afford to buy presents and he wasn't about to make them feel bad about it. So, as Alphonsine pushed the plate of pancakes towards him, he smiled his brightest smile.

'Now make a wish!' she urged. Colette, the poodle, yipped and nudged Frankie's hand. Frankie wasn't sure what to wish for. So he closed his eyes and, as he blew out the candles, he just wished that he would not have to spend another lunchbreak sitting on his own, staring at his trainers.

'Thank you,' smiled Frankie, 'this is going to be a great birthday.'

Alphonsine and Eddie exchanged mischievous glances.

'Well, don't you want to know what your present is?' said Eddie.

'But, I thought . . .' Frankie stammered, not sure what to say. Alphonsine put her fingers between her lips and gave a sharp whistle. Suddenly, a mechanical whirring sound started up from behind the sofa.

It couldn't be . . .

Could it . . . ?

Frankie could hardly believe his eyes. Hopping across the carpet on its mechanical paws was a sheeny blue Gadget the Rabbit.

'Frankie!' it crackled in its mechanical voice. *'Be my friend!'*

'But, Alfie . . .' said Frankie, 'we can't afford—'

'I find him at ze dump!' grinned Alphonsine. 'He was all dents and scratches and broken bits. Some children zey do not look after their things, tut, tut.' Alphonsine shook her head disapprovingly. 'But I

fix him up, good as gumdrops!' Frankie threw his arms around Alphonsine's neck. This really was going to be the greatest birthday ever.

Minutes later, Frankie was racing to school with his new Gadget the Rabbit in his rucksack. No more lunchbreaks sitting alone on the bench! No more teasing from Timmy Snodgrass! Not now that he had a Mechanimal! He sprinted across the playground to join his classmates, who were busy playing Spacestation Mechanimal near the climbing frame. Straight away, everybody crowded round to see Frankie's new toy.

'Wicked!' said Bernard. 'I really want a Gadget. I've got a Gigawatt, and a Sparky, but I *really* want a Gadget – he's the best!' Frankie's cheeks prickled with pleasure as his classmates started squabbling over who would have Frankie in their team for the Great Mechanimal Space-Battle. But not everybody was impressed. No. Somebody was not impressed at all.

'Let me see that!' Timmy Snodgrass, who had been skulking by the bushes, pushed his way through the crowd and snatched Gadget out of Frankie's hands.

'Hey!' yelled Frankie. 'Give it back!' But Timmy wasn't listening. He briskly turned Gadget upside-down and inspected the underside of his foot. Frankie glimpsed two scratchy little marks.

'Ha!' Timmy shouted triumphantly. 'Just as I thought!' He shoved the toy under Frankie's nose. Scratched on to the sole of Gadget's shiny blue foot were the letters 'TS –' *Timothy Snodgrass*.

'I chucked this out last week,' smirked Timmy. 'Mummy's getting me the new model. Generation two.'

'Ooooooohhh!' cooed the other children,

turning their attention back to Timmy. 'Generation twooooo!'

'Well, I . . .' Frankie stammered. He was *so* embarrassed he didn't know what to say. But Timmy had only just started to enjoy himself.

'How did you get hold of this anyway?' he sneered. 'I bet it was that weird old lady you live with.' Timmy's eyes glinted like a lizard's scales. 'My mummy's seen her at the dump, fetching bits of other people's rubbish. That must be where she got this – at the dump!' Timmy wrinkled up his lips as if he'd been chewing a Brussels sprout. 'It's disgusting.'

Frankie clenched his fists and his stomach tightened. He felt as if a ball of lightning were forming in his belly – a ball of pure, white-hot anger. Then, before he knew where he was, he hurled himself at Timmy, arms flailing like windmills.

'Fight! Fight! Fight!' chanted the other children. The two boys plunged to the ground, where they struggled and wrestled, kicking up huge clouds of dirt.

'Fight! Fight! Fight!' The crowd quickly swelled, but Frankie was so furious he could hardly hear them. Nor could he hear Mrs Pinkerton manically blowing her whistle.

'Frankie Blewitt! Timothy Snodgrass!' she yelped. 'In my office *NOW*!'

Frankie and Timmy sat in Mrs Pinkerton's office like a pair of muddy socks.

'He started it, Miss!' Timmy sniffled, blinking his eyes and trying to dredge up some nice fat tears. 'Frankie's *bullying* me.' Frankie couldn't believe his ears – the *lies*! The *unfairness*! But Mrs Pinkerton was not completely silly.

'That's enough, Timothy,' she said, looking

sternly over her silver-rimmed spectacles. 'I don't want to know who started it. You were both fighting, so you are both getting a detention for misbehaviour.' Now it was Timmy's turn not to believe his ears. Timmy had never, ever got a detention before in his whole life.

'But . . . but . . . but . . . Mrs Pinkerton . . .' he stammered.

'No buts!' snapped Mrs Pinkerton. 'Now go and get yourselves cleaned up or you'll be late for class.'

Frankie and Timmy sloped out of Mrs Pinkerton's office and walked silently to the boys' toilets to scrub up. As he was dabbing some mud off his shirt, Frankie heard a small, teary sniffle. He glanced sideways at Timmy, who was wiping his nose on the cuff of his jumper. For the first time, Frankie actually felt a little bit sorry for him.

'I'm sorry I hit you, Timmy,' he said. 'Can't we

just be friends?' Timmy drew himself upright and stared at Frankie with swollen, red eyes.

'Friends?' he spat. 'I'll never be your friend!' Then, lowering his voice to a mean little whisper, he added, 'And I'm going to make sure nobody else is either.' With that, he turned and stomped out of the loos with a face like an angry turnip.

Chapter Five
Frankie-No-Friends

When Frankie arrived at school the next morning, he wondered if he had forgotten to take a shower. As soon as they saw him coming, the other kids in his class turned away as if a foul stink had just wafted up their nostrils.

'Hey, Dave! Hey, Charlie!' Frankie waved to two of his classmates, 'What's up with everyone today?' Dave and Charlie glanced at each other awkwardly then looked at the ground.

'What's going on?' asked Frankie. 'Did I miss something?'

'Ummm,' Dave started. 'No, Frankie. It's just . . . we can't be your friends any more.'

Frankie felt his cheeks flush red. 'Why not?' he asked. 'What did Timmy say?'

Charlie shuffled his feet. 'He said that if we speak to you, he won't let us come over to his house to play.' Dave was so embarrassed he couldn't even look Frankie in the eye. 'I'm really sorry, Frankie, but he's got a Mechanimal racetrack you know, and . . .'

'I know,' Frankie replied sadly as the two boys shuffled guiltily away.

Frankie felt like a walking dustbin. He had never been so miserable. He thought about his best friends, Neet and Wes. He hadn't seen them for so long he'd almost forgotten what it was like to have friends. Frankie sighed and pushed his hands deep into his empty pockets. Had Wes stopped writing because he didn't want to be friends either? And what about Neet? Would she still be his pal when she came back to school?

He heard some whoops and cheers coming from near the climbing frame. A crowd of children was hopping up and down as Timmy, prince of the playground, let them take turns with his new remote-controlled Mechanicopter. Frankie turned around and trudged back across the playground, his heart sinking all the way down to the bottom of his wellies.

'Oh dear, you look glum,' said Eddie, the moment Frankie walked through the door that evening. 'Whatever is the matter?'

Alphonsine clasped Frankie's face between her hands and studied him carefully.

'You is right, Eddie,' said Alphonsine. 'A face like a soggy pancake. What is the bother, little cabbage?'

'Oh, nothing,' said Frankie, trying to sound cheerful. 'I'm just tired.' But Alfie and Eddie were far too old and far too wise to believe him. They sat him down on the sofa and made him a cup of hot chocolate while Colette gave his cheek a friendly lick.

'Spill the peas, Frankie,' smiled Alphonsine. So Frankie spilled all the peas he had. He told them about the teasing and the fight and Timmy Snodgrass and feeling like a walking dustbin. As he let all the words come tumbling out, Alphonsine nodded her grey head and patted him gently on the knee.

'Don't you worry, little cabbage,' she said kindly. 'You don't need this Timmy What's-his-face.'

'Snodgrass,' Frankie sighed.

'Exactly,' said Alphonsine. 'You do not need this Timmy Snotgrass.'

Frankie giggled. '*Snod*grass.'

'But zat is what I said!' grinned Alphonsine. 'Zis Timmy Snottypants is not a proper friend.' Frankie spluttered with laughter. 'Is that not right, Eddie?'

'That's right,' said Eddie. 'Proper friends don't behave like that, do they, Colette?' Colette yelped and gave Frankie another lick on the cheek.

'Proper friends,' Alphonsine continued, raising one finger in the air, 'is not like toys. You do not pick zem up and put zem down and get bored with zem. You do not swap zem or take zem to the dump when they get old. No! A proper friend is for life, not just for Christmas!'

'But . . . I don't have *any* friends,' said Frankie. 'Nobody wants to be my friend any more.'

'Nonsenses,' Alphonsine replied, squeezing his shoulders tightly. 'We is all your friends, is we not?' Eddie and Colette nodded vigorously. 'And we think you is fine and dandy as you are.'

Frankie looked around at the three kind, smiling faces. For that moment he felt as warm and safe as a bird in a nest.

By the time Frankie went to bed that night, he was so tired a brass band couldn't have kept him awake. So at first he couldn't work out whether what he saw was just an effect of his exhausted imagination.

It was at that time of the night when sleepers sink into the darkest depths of slumber. It was just at the moment when Frankie touched the bottom of the dark, watery world of dreams, that he had the oddest sensation. He felt a strange pressure on his chest and his ears filled with an uncomfortable electrical crackling. Opening his eyes wide, he saw that his bedroom was bathed in a weird blue light.

Perched on his chest, looking straight at him with swivelling mechanical eyes, was his Gadget the Rabbit, glowing like a blue beacon, sparks flying between his long mechanical ears.

Frankie screamed and jumped out of bed. Immediately, the blue light vanished and, by the time Alphonsine burst into his room waving a burglar-bashing tennis racket, everything looked perfectly normal. Gadget had tumbled to the floor and was lying on the rug like a completely normal toy.

'Where is he? Where's he hiding himself?' yelled Alphonsine, leaping round the room swinging her racket like a champion.

'There's nobody here, Alfie,' said Frankie, feeling bewildered. 'At least I don't think so.'

'Then why all this hollering and squallering, Frankie?' Alphonsine asked. 'It is bang-wallop in the middle of the night!'

'Sorry, Alfie, I think I had a bad dream. That's all.'

Alphonsine tucked him back into bed. 'Ah,' she said, nodding wisely, 'nightscares are terrible things.'

'Night*mares*,' Frankie corrected her, smiling.

'Yes, yes,' said Alphonsine, 'but lucky for us, nightscares are not real.'

'You're right,' said Frankie, as Alphonsine kissed him goodnight, 'nightscares aren't real.'

All the same, before Frankie turned out the light he picked up Gadget the Rabbit, put him in the bottom of his wardrobe, and shut the door.

CHAPTER SIX
WHERE'S WES?

Frankie stamped his feet and clapped his hands against the cold morning air as he waited for Mrs Pinkerton to blow the whistle. As usual, he was sitting on the bench, waiting for playtime to end. Never in a million years had Frankie thought he would actually prefer lessons to playtime, but when you have no one to play with, double Maths with Mr Gripe suddenly doesn't seem so bad.

'What are you doing over here?' said a bright, smiley voice.

Frankie looked up. 'Neet!' he cried. Frankie

sprang to his feet and gave his best friend a hug. 'You're back!'

Neet grinned. 'Good to see you, Frankie!' she smiled. 'Chickenpox is rubbish, by the way, don't try it.'

'I won't,' Frankie giggled. He was so glad to have Neet back again. Everything was better when she was around.

'Wanna go play with the others?' asked Neet. Frankie wasn't sure what to say.

'Errr . . . I think . . . um . . . no, not really,' he stammered.

'What's the matter?' Neet frowned.

'Well . . . nobody's talking to me. Timmy told them not to.' Frankie looked at his friend. 'And if he sees *you* talking to me, well . . .'

Neet's eyes went as round as ping-pong balls.

'Well what?' she said, folding her arms crossly. 'I'm not doing what Timmy Snotbags tells me to.

Oooh!' she growled, 'he gets right up my nose. Tell you what, I'm going over there right now and—'

'No, wait!' said Frankie, catching her arm. 'It's OK. Anyway . . .' Frankie shuffled awkwardly. 'I already walloped him once.'

'Really?' beamed Neet. 'Good for you, Frankie!' Frankie grinned. He was so, so glad that Neet was back.

'Have you heard from Wes?' he asked as they wandered across the playground to where Mrs Pinkerton was blowing the whistle for assembly. 'He's not been in touch with me since he went off to stay with his aunt.' Wes had been one of Frankie and Neet's closest allies. He was only seven but he was such a smartypants that he had been put into the same class as the older kids. He had been a real help to Frankie and Neet when there had been all that 'trouble' at the school the year before.

But now he had left and nobody seemed to quite know where he'd gone.

'No,' said Neet, shaking her head. 'Not a peep. Poor Wes, it's terrible, isn't it?'

'What do you mean?' said Frankie.

'Didn't you hear?' said Neet, surprised. 'His mum and dad went missing on safari. Nobody knows what happened to them.'

'That's awful!' gasped Frankie.

'You bet,' said Neet. 'Mrs Pinkerton told me he'd gone to stay with his Auntie Elvira, but Mrs Pinkerton didn't have the address. He must have left in a hurry.'

'That's weird,' frowned Frankie. 'Why wouldn't Wes tell us where he was going?'

'I know!' said Neet. 'And there's another thing too, Frankie. It probably doesn't matter, but I thought I should tell you.'

'What is it?'

‘Well,’ said Neet, ‘I heard that Snuffles escaped over the summer.’ Frankie stopped dead in his tracks.

For those of you who don’t know who Snuffles is, let me explain. As I said earlier, there had been an awful lot of ‘trouble’ at Frankie and Neet’s school. Back then Cramley Primary had been a very different place, a much, much scarier place called Crammar Grammar. The old headmaster, Dr Calus Gore, had been a mad scientist who used the school as his laboratory and the children as guinea-pigs. He had wanted to use his scientific wizardry to turn every child in the school into an exam-passing robot with his terrifying Brain-drain machine. But luckily Frankie, Neet and Wes had put a stop to his plans just in the nick of time. While they were at it, they accidentally turned the headmaster into a fluffy white rat called Snuffles – which was a bit of a bonus. Ever since,

Snuffles had been safely locked up in a cage in the first-year classroom. Or so Frankie had thought.

'How did he get out?' whispered Frankie, horrified.

'I don't know,' said Neet, 'but I don't suppose we need to worry.'

'Hmmm.' Frankie's brow crinkled up like a crisp. He wasn't so sure. He hadn't forgotten Dr Gore's hair-raising experiments on his classmates, or the time when the headmaster had locked him in a dark cupboard for hours on end. He hadn't forgotten Dr Gore's acid yellow eyes or his rasping voice. Dr Gore was as crackers as a parrot and as dangerous as a snake. But Neet was right, wasn't she? What harm could he possibly do now? Frankie shuddered and tried to shrug off the cold hand of fear that had gripped the nape of his neck.

'Come on, Frankie,' said Neet. 'We'll be late for assembly!'

CHAPTER SEVEN
TEDDY MANYWISHES

The assembly hall was abuzz with excitement. Children were whispering frantically and every now and then a little squeal trilled round the room. Even Mrs Pinkerton looked pinker than usual.

'What's all the fuss?' Frankie asked Neet, as their class filed in.

'No idea,' she replied, 'but stand back, that first-year's about to explode!'

Frankie looked at a little boy who was so excited Frankie actually thought he could see him swelling up like a party balloon.

Mrs Pinkerton stood up on stage and clapped her hands. 'Settle down, children!' she called over the dozens of bobbing heads. 'Settle down!' The room hushed quickly. 'We have a very special visitor here today.' Mrs Pinkerton beamed like a luminous flamingo. 'Can anybody tell me who it is?'

Dozens of hands shot into the air.

'Teddy Manywishes! Teddy Manywishes!' yelled a nursery tot unable to control herself any longer.

'Now now, Molly,' frowned Mrs Pinkerton, 'don't shout out. And who knows why Teddy Manywishes is here?'

'Toys!' yelled Molly, who was too crazed with excitement to listen. 'TOOOOOOOOOYS!'

Neet and Frankie giggled at Mrs Pinkerton, who was doing her best to look cross.

'Now as you all know, Teddy Manywishes is

the store mascot for our wonderful new toyshop, Marvella Brand's Happyland, and he is here this morning to tell you something very special. So I'd like you all to give him a big Cramley School welcome.'

'GOOD MORNING, TEDDY MANYWISHES,' chanted eighty small voices.

The lights turned a dim shade of green and an enormous teddy dressed as a genie appeared in a puff of shimmering smoke.

'Oooooooooohhhhh!' cooed the children, their eyes widening into round, sparkling pools. Teddy Manywishes took a low bow, a big furry smile on his big furry face.

'GOOD MORNING KIDS!' said the teddy, in a high cartoon-like voice that Frankie thought made him sound like a squirrel with a blocked nose. 'My name is Teddy Manywishes and I make children's wishes come true!' The enormous bear made a sweeping gesture with his paws and a burst of rainbow sparkles drizzled down over the gobsmacked children. 'Now, which of you kiddlywinks likes toys?' Dozens of hands shot into the air as the assembly hall erupted into shouts of '*Me! Me! I do! Me!*' Some of the children were so excited they were up on their feet, bouncing up and down like Mexican beans. Frankie wasn't sure he liked being called a kiddlywink but, as the air fizzed around him, he felt his worries dissolve like a spoonful of sherbet.

'Well, let's just see what ol' Teddy Manywishes can do.' The giant bear clapped his furry paws and – *SHAZZAM!* – a large pink envelope appeared between them.

'Oh, wow! Oh, wow!' gasped Neet, jiggling about in her chair.

'Now what's this?' piped Teddy Manywishes in his cheery, squeaky voice. The children held their breath as the bear drew out an even pinker card. 'Oh, my! It looks like an invitation! Who'd like to come up and read out what it says?'

Frankie found himself springing to his feet and waving his arms in the air.

'What's your name, little feller?'

Frankie couldn't believe it – Teddy Manywishes had picked him, HIM! Frankie burbled his name.

'Well, come along now, Frankie Blewitt, we're all waiting.'

Frankie dashed to the front before the teddy changed its mind. He took the card between his hands. It looked just like the party invitation that his cousin Amelia had sent him the year before – all pink and sparkly, and decorated with rainbows and unicorns. He took a deep breath and read it out loud:

'Miss Marvella Brand would like you, the children of Cramley Primary, to come to a party

at her new store. There will fun, games and surprises!'

The children of Cramley gasped with delight. Nothing this exciting had happened in Cramley-on-the-Crump since the giraffes escaped from Mr Jojo's circus and went stampeding down the high street.

'Carry on now, Frankie,' trilled the bear, staring down at him with his big furry face and blinking his enormous mechanical eyes. 'What else does it say?'

Frankie felt slightly unnerved by this huge smiling face hovering above him like a fuzzy balloon. Or was he just overexcited? He could no longer tell. He continued reading:

'You will spend the whole day at my magical Happyland before taking home a toy of your choice!

'Lots of love and kisses

'Marvella XXX'

Frankie's heart was beating like a hamster's as the children whooped and cheered around him.

'You can sit down now, Master Blewitt,' said the teddy in his strange, squeaky voice. But Frankie was so dizzy with excitement he hardly heard him.

But not everyone was as excited as the schoolchildren of Cramley Primary. Alphonsine hummed and hawed and wrinkled her nose as Frankie told her about the visit over dinner.

'I do not trust it,' Alfie sniffed, mopping up some sauce with a crust of bread. 'I do not like it. I am most suspishy. Why would a toy*shop* be giving toys away? They must want something. They must be up to something. I smell a fish!'

'You smell a *rat*,' Frankie grumbled, disappointed that Alfie couldn't see how great it would be to spend a WHOLE DAY at Marvella's.

He might even get his hands on a Mechanimal Generation Three.

'Yes, yes,' said Alphonsine, 'there is something very ratty about it. I do not like it at all.'

'Alphonsine is right.' Eddie nodded. 'I wouldn't put much past Marvella Brand. I'd stay away from that toyshop if I were you.' Frankie poked at his dinner, crossly. He didn't see what was so very ratty about it. But, all the same, Alphonsine's doubts left a niggle in Frankie's mind. A niggle that he couldn't quite shake, however hard he tried.

CHAPTER EIGHT
THE PENCIL

As Class 5C made their way to the playground, Neet reached into the inside pocket of her blazer.

'I got a card from Wes this morning,' she said. Frankie's eyes lit up.

'How is he?' asked Frankie. 'Is he coming to visit soon?' Neet passed Frankie the card. The front showed a picture of a jolly-looking Father Christmas overseeing his elves as they loaded his sleigh with toys.

'It's a bit early for Christmas cards, isn't it?' said Frankie. 'It's only October.'

'Right,' said Neet. 'It's weird. And it doesn't sound like Wes at all.' Frankie opened the card and read. 'Dear Neet and Frankie, I am at my Auntie Elvira's. It is raining non-stop. Everything is soaking wet. Hope to see you soon. Wes.'

Neet was right. It was nothing like Wes's usual notes and letters. There were no jokes or wacky ideas, only the kind of boring stuff you write when you can't think of anything to say.

'It's like someone else has written it,' said Frankie, 'and there is no return address.'

Frankie frowned and started to reread the card. But he didn't get very far.

'No playtime for you, Frankie Blewitt!' Mrs P was blocking his path. 'You and Timmy are on detention, remember?'

Frankie hated detention. Who doesn't? While Neet was outside in the autumn sunshine, he had to sit in the classroom with Timmy Snotbags and write 'I MUST NOT START FIGHTS' one hundred times over. *Urrgh! So unfair!* thought Frankie. *I didn't start it, Timmy did. I never would have hit him if he hadn't been such a twazzock, and anyway* . . . But there was no point arguing. He had been sentenced to spend the lunchbreak at his desk, so he picked up his pencil and got on with it.

Timmy was in a funny mood. He had been ignoring Frankie all week, but that afternoon he seemed strangely pleasant.

'Could I borrow your spare pencil, Frankie?' Timmy asked politely.

'Okaaaay,' Frankie replied, 'but I've only got this green one.'

'That's perfect,' said Timmy with a smile. 'Listen, Frankie,' he continued in his most grown-up voice, 'shall we put it all behind us – let bygones be bygones?'

Frankie wondered if he had cleaned his ears out properly. But Timmy seemed to be serious.

'Uhh . . . sure, Timmy!' Frankie smiled, relieved. 'I'd like that.'

The boys sat in silence for half an hour, diligently copying out their lines. Frankie had been stuck in detention so many times before that he had perfected a method of writing lines that made it as quick and painless as possible. He would start by writing 'I' over and over again down the margin, followed by 'MUST', followed by 'NOT', and so on. Try it next time you're in detention, it takes half the time, I promise.

'I'll take them down to Mrs Pinkerton's office,' Timmy offered once time was up, handing back Frankie's pencil.

'Thanks, Timmy,' Frankie replied. 'That's nice of you.' Timmy smiled a small compressed smile that made his mouth look like a squeezed lemon, snatched Frankie's worksheet and hurried out of the classroom.

Later that afternoon, Frankie was sitting in his Science lesson, designing a gadget for getting spiders out of the bath and dreaming about the trip to Marvella's, when a furious Mrs Pinkerton burst into the classroom. Frankie had never seen her so cross. She had turned such an alarming shade of fuchsia it was hard to tell where her jumper ended and her face began. *Uh oh, somebody's in trouble,* thought Frankie, glad to have got his detention over with.

'Frrrankie BLEWITT!'

Frankie looked up from his desk, confused.

'I supposed you think this is funny!'

Mrs Pinkerton slapped a worksheet down in front of him. Sure enough it had Frankie's name at the top, but underneath it, in his very own bright green pencil were the words: 'MRS

STINKERTON PICKS HER NOSE AND EATS IT' written out exactly one hundred times.

Frankie gasped. 'I didn't write that, Mrs Stink— I mean, Pinkerton! Timmy must have switched the papers! He must have put my name at the top! I didn't do it, I promise!'

'That's a lie!' cried Timmy triumphantly. 'Look!' Timmy grabbed Frankie's pencil case and showed Mrs Pinkerton and the class the offending green pencil as if he were a lawyer presenting evidence to the jury.

'Well that settles it!' squawked Mrs Pinkerton. 'I've had quite enough of your naughtiness, Frankie! You obviously can't behave yourself so I have no choice but to exclude you from our school trip to Marvella's.'

The class gasped in horror. Never before had such a ghastly punishment been dished out to a pupil of Cramley Primary.

'In fact,' flushed Mrs Pinkerton, 'you can collect your things and go home right now. I've had enough of you for one day.' Frankie opened and closed his mouth like the class goldfish. He was so shocked he could not think of a word to say, not even to that sneaky, cheating, double-bluffing trickster, Timothy Snotgrass.

'But that's not fair, Mrs Pinkerton!' said Neet, getting out of her chair.

'Sit down right away, young lady!' squawked Mrs Pinkerton. 'Or I'll exclude you too.'

'It's all right, Neet,' said Frankie, collecting his things together as fast as he could. 'You go. I'll see you on Friday.' He could feel the tears beginning to burn behind his eyes. The last thing he wanted was for the whole class to see him cry. Frankie gulped back a sob, grabbed his protractor and ran out of the classroom, disappointment crushing his chest like a python.

CHAPTER NINE
THE PYJAMAS

The next morning Frankie woke up with a soupy feeling in his belly. As he lay on his bed, it seemed to be swaying slightly, as if it were adrift on the sea. Frankie opened one heavy eyelid and peered blearily around him. The objects in his bedroom slowly settled into their usual places and his bed seemed to steady. But Frankie still had a strong sense that something was not right. Something strange had happened. Something in the night. Something that he couldn't quite remember. Frankie stayed motionless under his blankets. He had the impression that if he moved, even slightly, he would break the delicate threads that connected the new day to the world of sleep. But if he could follow those threads back into the labyrinth of the night maybe, just maybe, he would remember what had happened. Frankie's eye alighted on his cupboard door. It stood slightly ajar. Did he leave it like that? He felt the trickle of a memory filter into his imagination. Then it all came flooding back . . .

In the dead of night Frankie had awoken (or so he thought) to see Gadget the Rabbit hopping through his bedroom door. Frankie rubbed his eyes to check he wasn't seeing things, but no, there was Gadget, hopping on to the landing as if it had a life of its own. Frankie shuddered. He didn't know what his rabbit was up to but a chill in his bones told him it was up to no good. No good at all. He slipped out of bed as quietly as a

moth, slid his feet into his slippers and followed. Peering around the door frame, Frankie saw his toy rabbit bouncing down the stairs, a faint crackling issuing from its long mechanical ears. He followed on quickly and quietly, making as little noise as possible, as the mechanical toy hopped down to the kitchen, skipped smartly across the tiles, then leapt through the catflap and headed towards the end of the garden.

Frankie's heart was thumping like a drum as he stepped quietly into the damp night. He dropped to his hands and knees to avoid being seen and crawled quickly behind the nearest shrub. From where he was hiding, Frankie saw the rabbit leap up on to the roof of the garden shed, stand on its hind legs and point its ears skywards. Then it began to swivel them around as if trying to pick up a signal – left, right, left, right – it seemed to be seeking something far off in the distance. *What on earth is it doing?* Frankie wondered. *Who or what is Gadget trying to communicate with?*

The crackling sound turned into a series of pips and long beeps. Gadget had found what it was looking for. The beeps grew louder and the toy glowed a bright luminous blue as the tips of his ears began to send pulses of light out into the night sky. Frankie frowned. Gadget wasn't receiving, it was transmitting. It was sending signals to something, to someone, way off in the distance. But who? The pulses grew more powerful and frequent. The same rhythm of pips and beeps, over and over again, rippling through the night like a wave machine. As he felt the waves pass through his body, Frankie felt quite sick. He flattened himself against the damp grass and jammed his fingers in his ears . . .

That was all Frankie could remember. He rubbed his head and crawled out from under his blankets. Daylight was now flooding through the window giving the objects in his room a reassuring brightness. He walked to the cupboard and opened it cautiously. There was Gadget, propped up neatly on the shelf. Frankie picked him up and inspected him. He seemed as plastic and lifeless as any other factory toy. Frankie sighed. 'Another nightscare,' he said to himself out loud, 'just another nightscare.' Frankie stretched out his arm to place Gadget back in the cupboard, but as he did so something caught his eye. Something that made his heart stop still. On the elbow of his pyjama top was a patch of muddy green. Frankie looked down at his trousers. There were two more patches just below the knee. Grass stains.

CHAPTER TEN
PROJECT WISHLIST

Alphonsine sucked thoughtfully on her morning coffee as Frankie breathlessly explained what he had seen in the night.

'Slow down, Frankie!' said Eddie, feeding Colette a sneaky strip of bacon under the table. 'I can hardly catch a word!'

'Sorry,' said Frankie, taking a deep breath. 'But you see what I'm saying, right?' Alphonsine inspected the grass stains closely.

'You say ze bunny was peeping and blipping.'

'Pipping and bleeping, yes,' said Frankie.

'And do you remember what it sounded like?'

Frankie had no trouble remembering the sequence. It was as if it had been printed on his eardrums. He hummed it out loud for Alphonsine to hear. Alphonsine narrowed her grey old eyes and pursed her lips so tightly you could have sharpened a pencil between them.

'Something most fishy is afloat,' she muttered. Eddie nodded in agreement. 'I do not know what it is. But I have not smelt anything this fishy since Colette gobbled Mrs Popper's kippers.' Colette blushed with shame.

'Why do you say that, Alfie?' asked Frankie.

'Ze rabbit was sending messages in morse code. It is a very simple code of bips and pleeps. I learnt it during ze war. Very good for sending tip-top secret messages.'

'What was Gadget saying?' asked Frankie, alarmed that his toy bunny could do such a thing.

'It said, *"Project Wishlist – stage one complete"*.'

'But what does that mean?' said Frankie, trying to get his head around what had happened.

'I haven't the foggiest,' said Eddie, 'but I'll tell you one thing. That Marvella is not to be trusted. We need to look into this.'

'True!' said Alphonsine, holding a finger in the air. 'We must go to the Marvella shop and sniff it out.'

'But it doesn't open till tomorrow,' said Frankie, 'and today is the school visit. I don't have permission to be there.'

'Permission?' scoffed the old spy. 'Pffff! We is working tip-top secret undercover! We do not need nonsenses like *permission*. We must be silent. We must be stealthy. We must rummage in the dustbins.'

'Rummage in the dustbins?' said Frankie, wrinkling up his nose.

'But of course!' said Alphonsine, widening her eyes at such a silly question. 'Dustbins is the best place to start. People is always throwing away things they don't want anyone to see.'

'No one knows how to rummage through a bin like my Alphonsine,' said Eddie, adoringly.

'All right then,' said Frankie, finishing off his breakfast. 'Let's go!'

As Alphonsine parked her motorbike in a quiet side road, Frankie pulled off his helmet and looked up at the towering toy palace that dwarfed the street and the surrounding village. Frankie felt a knot tightening in his stomach.

'No time to be wasting!' said Alphonsine, clapping her hands together. 'Colette will keep watch out.' The poodle sat up to attention and flicked her beady eyes from side to side. 'I will rummage in ze bins – and Frankie, you can sneak about, eyes agoggle, looking for ways in. We meet back here in ten minutes. Find out what you can.'

Frankie crouched behind a skip and checked out the back of the building. As he searched for a way in, he noticed how much the back of Marvella Brand's Happyland differed from the front. While the shop front was a fantastical dream castle topped with fluttering flags, the back was an imposing block of glass and steel bristling with swivelling satellite dishes. And while the front of the store was guarded by a smiley pair of red-cheeked toy soldiers, the back was patrolled by dozens of unblinking security cameras tracking back and forth across the car park. Frankie could not see a single chink in the cold, smooth wall that towered over him. His best bet, he thought, would be to scale the fire escape at the side. From there, he would be able to peer in through the windows.

Frankie pulled up his hood to shield his face from the roving mechanical eyes and made a dash for the bottom of the stairway. His heart was pounding like a locomotive as he cupped his hands around his face and peered through the ground-floor window. Through the smoky glass, Frankie made out a series of flickering television monitors displaying images from security cameras inside the store. He felt a sudden jolt of sadness as he recognised his classmates on the monitors. There was Dave and Charlie playing in the Super-Spy section. And there was Joseph and Alice trying out the rocket-propelled rollerskates. The images changed and Frankie recognised Neet. She was standing on her own by the Mechanimals, quietly looking through some accessories. Frankie sighed. He still wished he could join them, but there wasn't much time and he needed to do some proper snooping.

He kept moving up the stairs. The blinds of the first and second floors were shut tight, blocking his view. As he pressed his face against the glass of the third-floor window he began to wonder whether he should turn back and look for another way. But no, this time he was in luck. The window stood ajar and the blinds were tilted slightly, allowing Frankie to see through a narrow crack. On the other side of the glass was an enormous office. People in smart suits swarmed about like ants in a nest, shouting down their phones or tapping furiously at keyboards. Frankie could make out a few words here and there over the general hubbub. 'I want this done yesterday!' yelled a man with a face like a beetroot.

'Failure is not an option!' shouted another.

Frankie pulled away from the window as a woman with a tightly-scraped bun glided dangerously close. She was speaking to a younger, bewildered-looking colleague. 'They may be children,' she sneered, 'but they are also customers. Don't forget that.' She then led her colleague over to a wall covered with charts and diagrams and pointed to one that appeared to show a cross-section of a child's brain. Printed above it was a single question: '*What do children want?*' Frankie felt confused. It all seemed so different from the magical world of Marvella's. Where were the smiling faces and merry tunes? He wanted to get the jiminy out of there. But there was one more floor to see.

Frankie took a deep breath and climbed the final flight of stairs right to the top of the building. It was a long way up and he was starting to feel slightly queasy. As he neared the top floor he saw that the roof was sprouting with twitching antennae and swivelling satellite dishes and he began to feel a heavy pulsing in his temples, like he did whenever a storm was gathering. Frankie approached the windows and squinted through the dark glass. At first he thought he had stumbled across another security office. Dozens, maybe hundreds, of TV monitors flickered on the high walls. But there were no security guards. Instead, stern-looking men and women, each wearing a large set of headphones, were watching the screens through narrowed eyes and pushing buttons on an enormous control panel. It was an enormous computer laboratory but far more high-tech than anything he had ever seen. Frankie strained his eyes to try to make sense of the rapidly-moving images on the screens.

One thing was for sure, these images had not been filmed by security cameras. The monitors displayed scenes that looked as if they had been taken from family movies or photo albums. There were holidays, birthday parties and days at the beach but there were also more everyday images. There was a child with grazed knees being comforted by his dad, and another in which two small girls were reading comics and rolling around in fits of giggles. All of these scenes seemed to give off a warm, magical glow. But the people in the headphones didn't seem to notice. They just rewound and replayed the tapes, squinting at the children on the monitors as if they were tadpoles in a jar. But some of the monitors showed other things. Things that made Frankie gulp with sadness or sweat with fright. There were scenes of a small boy being told off for something he hadn't done, and a sequence in which a girl wandered across a park at twilight, lost and howling with terror.

Then, all of a sudden, Frankie saw something that shook him rigid. On one screen, there for everyone to see, was a ten-year-old boy sitting alone on a bench as the other children played together at the end of the playground. Frankie felt as if the air had been sucked out of his lungs. His head was pounding and he felt the same swilling, soupy feeling in his stomach that he had felt the night before. He lurched away from the glass and staggered down the fire escape as fast as he could.

He found Alphonsine rummaging headfirst in a huge bin, tossing promising-looking scraps to Colette.

'We've got to get out of here,' said Frankie. 'Quickly.'

'What is it?' said Alphonsine, pulling a bit of cabbage out of her hair. 'What did you find out?'

Frankie took a deep breath. 'I think I know what's wrong with my Mechanimal.'

Chapter Eleven
Mind-Sweepers

Neet Banerjee sat on her own on the bus back from Marvella's. Since she'd come back to school her old friends Millie and Miranda weren't talking to her. They had said that if she wanted to stay in their *Best Friends Forever Club* then she'd have to stop hanging out with that loser Frankie, at which point Neet had told them that she didn't give a monkeynut about their club, and that was the end of that. She didn't regret it for a second, but all the same it was horrid to be left out.

To cheer herself up, Neet rummaged through

the loot in her goody-bag. There was an *I Love Marvella's* T-shirt and an *I Love Marvella's* badge, but best of all there was a Gadget the Rabbit schoolbag that she had picked out especially for Frankie. It had a pair of shiny rabbit ears sticking out of the top and a billion different pockets to keep all your gadgets and gizmos in. As Neet was inspecting the different zips and flaps she suddenly saw something that didn't look like it was supposed to be there. Sticking out of one of the inside pockets was a slip of creased paper. Neet pulled it out and carefully unfolded it. It was a message. Neet smoothed out the creases so that she could see it clearly. The words were written in a large spidery scrawl as if the writer had been in a terrible hurry. Suddenly, she drew a sharp gasp. She knew that handwriting.

As soon as the bus pulled over, Neet jumped out, ran as fast as she could to Frankie's house and hammered on the door

'Frankie,' she blurted, waving the note in the air, 'I found this! I think Wes wrote it! Something's wrong!' Frankie took the note and read the two trembling words out loud: '*HELP US!*'

'Good grief!' said Frankie. 'I think you're right. It really does look like Wes's writing. Nobody else joins up their letters like that.' Alphonsine took the note and turned it between her fingers.

'Most fishy,' she mumbled. 'There is something most stinky going on at Marvella's, my friends, no doubts about it.' Eddie nodded in agreement as Colette growled softly.

'What do you mean?' asked Neet. 'What's going on?'

They gathered round the kitchen table and Frankie described all the strange things that he had seen through the windows of Marvella's – the diagram of the child's brain, the swivelling satellite dishes and, strangest of all, the spooky images in the computer lab.

'It was *me*, Neet,' he whispered. 'It was me, sitting on my own in the playground. It was like they sucked the thoughts right out of my brain.'

'But that is exactly what they did!' said Alphonsine with certainty. 'Watch this.' Alphonsine whipped her screwdriver out of her apron pocket, seized Frankie's Gadget the Rabbit and set about unscrewing the panel at the back of the toy's head. 'Look!' said Alphonsine, pointing at the complicated circuitry inside. 'This is not a toy. This is a mind-sweeper!' Alphonsine fished about in the back of Gadget's head with a pair of tweezers and pulled out what looked like a miniature crystal ball. 'You see this little wotsit here . . .' Neet nodded. '. . . It is for snitching your thoughts, dreams and memories, everything that you is keeping between your ears!'

Neet gulped and examined the tiny crystal ball, which looked as if it were filled with trapped lightning.

'Our Mechanimals have been reading our minds in our sleep,' Frankie explained, peering at the long, flexing sparks that clawed the glass like electrical fingers. 'They have been burgling our brains, collecting all our thoughts then beaming them back to the computer lab at Marvella's.'

'But why would they do that?' She frowned. 'And how is Wes mixed up in all of this? Poor Wes! What's happened to him?'

'*That*, my friends,' said Alphonsine, scratching her nose in thought, 'is what we must be finding out.'

CHAPTER TWELVE
The Grotto

Frankie and Neet watched from a distance as Lady Buntley-Bottom, the Mayoress, declared Marvella Brand's Happyland officially open. No sooner had she snipped the ribbon than hordes of children and parents stampeded through the golden doors like buffalo into a waterhole.

'Right,' said Frankie, pulling up his hood, 'we need to go in and have a proper snoop round. Find out what we can. Anything at all that might tell us what's going on. Anything that could help us find Wes.'

'Got it,' Neet replied. 'You take the ground floor, I'll go upstairs. Ready?' The two friends took a deep breath, then plunged into the crowds.

The throng of people inside the shop was so dense that Frankie could hardly breathe. The crowd pushed him this way and that as children and parents scrambled to get their hands on the most popular toys. Over the blaring of the loudspeakers and the ringing of the tills rose shrieks of excitement, but also howls of disappointment as the most-wanted toys sold out.

'They'll have some more in next week,' said one tired-looking mum trying to calm down a damp-faced little girl. 'We'll come back then.' But the girl didn't stop bawling. A whole week! A week was forever!

Frankie worked his way towards the edge of the store where the crowds were a little thinner so that he could get a proper view of the inside of the store. Frankie gasped. The inside was even more spectacular than the outside. The high ceilings left space for dozens of remote-control birds, helicopters and rockets zipping and dipping high over his head. But the Mechanimals were, of course, the star attraction. A giant Sparky the Squirrel, three times Frankie's height, swivelled forward, blinking its eyes, and making a mechanical chuckling noise, while an enormous Gigawatt plodded slowly through the centre of the store, roaring and swishing its tail.

Frankie heard a familiar beeping sound behind him. He turned to see a colossal Gadget the Rabbit bearing down on him, twitching its enormous mechanical nose. Frankie shrieked in alarm before toppling backwards into a vat of squeaky foam balls.

'Ha ha ha!' Poppy Malone, a freckly first-year

from Cramley, was pointing at Frankie and clutching her sides in laughter. 'Scaredy-cat!' she shrieked. 'It's just a toy, you know!'

'That's what *you* think,' Frankie muttered under his breath as he hauled himself squeakily back on to his feet. The giant rabbit was amusing a group of children by clapping its steely paws. Frankie narrowed his eyes. 'That's what everybody thinks.'

Frankie dusted himself down and sloped away, keeping his hood up and his head low to avoid the gaze of the security cameras. As he neared the back of the shop, he noticed that a section had been roped off. He went over to inspect. Beyond the rope was a glittering cave surrounded by twinkling lights and flanked by life-size toy reindeer. Santa's Grotto! *They must be getting it ready for Christmas,* thought Frankie. The mouth of the cave was dark and deep and seemed to go back a long way. Frankie looked behind him to check no one was watching, but luckily the whole store seemed transfixed by a magic show that had just started in the Witches and Wizards section. This was his chance. He slid under the rope and disappeared into the cave mouth like water down a drain.

It took a while for Frankie's eyes to adjust to the darkness and even then he could only make out the vaguest shapes as he ventured deep into the gaping gullet of the cave. The hubbub of the shop faded away until all he could hear was the sound of his own breathing. He gulped nervously. Maybe he should go back. Was he really going to find anything in there? But his feet kept moving forward in spite of him. Suddenly a small face surfaced through the gloom. Frankie stifled a scream – it was only a mannequin. He rubbed his eyes and stared into the near-darkness. All around him were models of smiling elves in a mock workshop making toys for Santa's sleigh. But each one of them was as still as stone, as if under some malevolent spell.

Frankie was beginning to feel the cold fingers of fear creep across the back of his neck when, all of a sudden, he had a strong sense that he was being watched. Was it the twinkling eyes of the elves? Had he heard something moving in the darkness? He couldn't tell. But his gut told him that there was somebody else in the grotto. 'Hello?' whispered Frankie nervously. 'Is there someone here? . . . Wes?'

There was a scuffling sound behind him then a dash of footsteps. Whoever it was was making a getaway. Frankie spun round to see two small flashing lights.

'Hey!' Frankie shouted, summoning up all his courage. 'Hey! Come back!' The lights were heading for the exit. Frankie took a deep breath and gave chase. He could hardly see where he was going as he stumbled through the darkness . As he turned a corner he saw the pair of lights disappear through some heavy curtains. But before he caught up, he tripped and crashed to the floor, striking his head sharply on the way down. The grotto sprang instantly to life. Jingling Christmas music and loud ho ho hos filled the air as grinning animatronic elves loaded Santa's sleigh with presents. Frankie was so dizzy the whole grotto seemed to be swirling around him. The ground shifted and swayed as if he were on the deck of a ship. He staggered to his feet, clutching his thumping head, and fumbled towards the exit. He could make out a large illuminated sign but his vision was so blurred that the letters would not settle into a readable pattern. There was a C and an A and an L . . .

There was a G . . . and an O . . . and . . . He gasped in horror. In his groggy state, the letters spelt out the name of someone Frankie hoped he would never meet again. His worst and most dreadful enemy: DR CALUS GORE. Then his eyes seemed to fill with blackness and he passed out on the spot.

CHAPTER THIRTEEN
THE LIGHTS

'Wake up! Frankie! Wake up!'

Neet was shaking him vigorously as if he were a bottle of ketchup.

'Owwwwww,' murmured Frankie as he came round. He put his hand to his pounding head and felt a lump the size of an egg. 'It's OK, Neet,' he said. 'I think I'm OK.' As Frankie looked up, his blurry vision caught sight of some large illuminated letters: '*SANTA CLAUS'S GROTTO*'. *Of course*, thought Frankie, shaking his head, *'Claus' not 'Calus'*.

He breathed a deep sigh of relief.

'You sure you're all right, Frankie?' said Neet.

'I'm fine,' Frankie replied, staggering to his feet. 'My eyes were playing tricks on me, that's all.' Frankie forced out a laugh, but he could not quite untwist the knot that had formed in his stomach.

When they got home, Alphonsine and Eddie fussed over him like a couple of hens. 'Here,' said Eddie, spooning some honey-coloured liquid into Frankie's mouth. 'I mixed up this medicine this morning. It should make the swelling go down.'

'My Eddie's medicines always do the biscuit,' said Alphonsine proudly.

'Do the business,' whispered Frankie, still feeling terribly woozy.

'Yes, yes,' muttered Alphonsine, 'same thing.'

'I found him in Santa's grotto,' Neet explained.

'He was knocked out on the floor. What happened in there, Frankie?'

Frankie closed his eyes and tried to remember. Slowly, shreds of memory floated to the surface. He remembered the reindeer and the strange, grinning faces of the elves. Then he remembered the pair of lights.

'There was somebody in there with me,' said Frankie. 'I don't know who, but they were watching me and then I heard them run out. There were two flashing lights. I tried to run after them and that's when I tripped and hit my head.'

Neet frowned and folded her arms. 'I see,' she said.

'What is it, Neety?' asked Alphonsine.

'Timothy Snodgrass,' Neet replied with certainty.

'What makes you say that?' said Frankie.

'He's got these new trainers,' said Neet. 'He's

been showing them off to everyone at school – they have lights on the heel that flash different colours as he walks. I think they're called Glo-Getters.'

'Oh they're awesome!' smiled Frankie, perking up. 'I can't believe Timmy's got some already! They only came out last week!'

'Ahem!' coughed Alphonsine. 'Ze question is, what was Timmy Snotgrass doing in ze grotto?'

'I didn't think much of it till now,' Neet frowned, 'but he's been acting a bit strangely lately. Ever since our trip to Marvella's.'

'What do you mean?' asked Frankie.

'Yesterday he kept sitting next to me in class. Then later, I startled him when I went into the cloakroom to get my bag. I thought he had been rummaging through it, but I couldn't be sure. In any case, it wouldn't surprise me if he were up to something.'

'Hmmm,' Alphonsine murmured, tugging pensively on a wiry white hair sprouting from her chin. 'He is watching you. He is following. But why?'

'Well there is only one way to find out,' groaned Frankie, heaving himself off the sofa. 'If he's been spying on us, we need to start spying on him!'

'Not so fast, young man.' Eddie pushed Frankie gently back onto the sofa. 'How's your head?'

'Oh much better thanks,' smiled Frankie. The swelling had already gone down to half the size and the honey mixture had given Frankie a lovely warm feeling in his belly.

'Spying, eh?' Alphonsine muttered mysteriously. 'I have exactly ze thing you need – exactly ze thing.' She disappeared up the stairs while the others waited in the living room. Then, after a great deal of crashing about in the attic, she reappeared carrying a battered metal trunk, dented and covered with dirt as if it had once been buried under the roots of a tree.

'What's that, Alfie?' said Neet. 'What's in it?'

Alphonsine cast suspicious sideways glances as if she were afraid of being seen, then prised off the lid. Frankie and Neet peered eagerly inside. But all they saw was a motley collection of bits and bobs – the sort of stuff you might find at a car boot sale. Amongst the junk was a couple of bent pairs of spectacles, a bunch of old shoes, and a tarnished perfume bottle on a chain. But Alphonsine was looking at them with sparkling eyes, as if they were her most precious possessions.

'This is my treasure-box!' she whispered excitedly.

Frankie was struggling to see what was so special about these odds and ends. He picked up a watch.

'That,' Alphonsine announced proudly, 'is a *watcher*!'

'A watch,' corrected Neet.

'No, no, a watcher,' Alphonsine repeated, 'for *watching*. Look!' Alphonsine pressed the wind-up mechanism at the side. Immediately the watch face sprang open and a miniature camera popped out and snapped a picture. Neet and Frankie blinked in wonder. 'Eyes for spies!' sang Alphonsine delightedly. 'When Eddie and I were in ze Resistance, during ze war, many years ago, it was our job to spy on ze enemy. This is our box of tricks!'

'Woooooow!' cooed Frankie. This was so much better than all those fake spy-gadgets at Marvella's.

Frankie picked up a pair of scruffy-looking shoes. 'Put zem on,' grinned Alphonsine. Frankie did as he was told. 'Now run around ze room.'

Frankie took a few steps across the wooden

floorboards then stopped in astonishment. Normally the aged floorboards would creak and groan underfoot, but this time Frankie's footsteps were as silent as a cat's.

'Silent sneakers!' said Alphonsine proudly, lifting Frankie's foot and pressing on the padded sole. 'For sneaking about – top of ze range!' She threw a second pair to Neet while Frankie took out the perfume bottle and tossed it lightly in his hand.

'Watch out!' warned Alphonsine. 'It'll go off!'

Frankie froze.

'You . . . you mean it's a bomb?' he stammered.

'But of course!' chortled Alphonsine. 'A smoke-bomb. Pull off ze chain and – *whoooooooosh!* Smoke everywhere! Very good for getaways.' Frankie breathed a sigh of relief and placed the bottle gently on the carpet. Neet held up a pair of cloudy spectacles.

'And what about these sunglasses?' asked Neet.

'*Moon*glasses,' corrected Alphonsine, reaching over to the lampshade and switching off the light. 'Try zem!'

Neet slipped them on to her nose and blinked. The room was in darkness but Neet could see everything as if the place were flooded with the clearest moonlight.

'Night vision!' she cooed. 'Wow!'

Alphonsine demonstrated her other gadgets. There was a pen that wrote in invisible ink, an umbrella that turned inside out to become a radio receiver, and an old granny-shawl that opened up into a full-scale parachute.

'A para-shawl!' said Alphonsine proudly. 'I invented this one myself. Pull these tassels here, and – *whoooosh!*' Alphonsine flung her arms out wide. 'You are floating like a jellyfish. Cunning, is it not?'

Frankie looked at all the extraordinary gadgets strewn across the carpet and drew a deep breath. It was cunning indeed, very cunning. But they were going to have to be more than cunning if they were to find their friend Wes.

'Take what you need,' said the old spy. 'But listen very carefully. Spying is not a game. It is a very risky business. You must be patient and you must be brave. You never know what you might find out.'

CHAPTER FOURTEEN
MARVELLA BRAND

Neet had been right about Timmy. The next day, Frankie noticed him behaving very oddly indeed. Usually Timmy didn't want to be seen anywhere near Frankie-no-friends but that day he seemed to be lurking around every corner.

'Have you heard any more from Wes?' Frankie asked Neet, as they queued up for their lunch.

'Shhh,' whispered Neet, flashing a warning glance. 'He's listening.' Frankie peered over his shoulder and, sure enough, there was Timmy pretending he was studying the ceiling. Then later on, when he and Neet were eating their crisps on the playground bench, Frankie heard a rustling in the bushes behind him.

'Timmy!' Neet whispered and, lo and behold, there was Timmy scurrying away with a notepad and pencil.

'Alphonsine's right,' said Frankie, shaking his head. 'He's spying on us. Let's just hope we're better at it than he is!'

They didn't have to wait long to find out. As the children drained out of the school gates Frankie and Neet kept a close eye on their target. Then, as soon as Timmy had left the school grounds, they started to follow. Before long it was clear that Timmy was not on his way home. He took off in the opposite direction, walking hurriedly along the pavements and staying close to the walls.

Soon they were beyond the houses and

heading out of town. The light was fading fast as the autumn sun sank beyond the horizon, but the two trackers were grateful for the cover of darkness. Timmy scurried on like a worried beetle, clutching his rucksack to his shoulders. He led them over the heath, then on past an abandoned playground. Frankie shuddered to see the broken swings and the rusted roundabout. Suddenly a frightening thought occurred to him. 'Do you think he knows we're here?' Frankie whispered anxiously. 'What if he is leading us somewhere?'

Neet shook her head. 'I don't think so, Frankie,' she said. 'But if we want to find Wes then it's a chance we have to take.' Frankie nodded and they pushed on.

Timmy led them up a steep winding road. They were close enough to hear the thud and crunch of his footsteps but, thanks to Alphonsine's silent sneakers, their own feet didn't make a sound.

'Urrgh! How much farther?' puffed Neet as the road climbed sharply. Then, as they came around the bend, their eyes widened with amazement.

Perched on top of the hill was what looked like an enormous doll's house. The walls were straight and square, the windows gleamed like glassy eyes, and *everything* was a shade of bubblegum pink.

'Ewwww,' groaned Neet. 'I haaaate pink!' But there was no escaping it – the door was pink, the walls were pink, even the tiles on the roof were pink. The friends hid themselves behind a perfectly pink rose-bush and watched Timmy scuttle quickly up the path and ring the doorbell. The candy-coloured door opened quickly but, from where they were hiding, Neet and Frankie could not see who was behind it. Then, as Timmy stepped inside, they heard a peal of laughter that sounded like the jingle of coins.

'Quickly,' urged Frankie, making a dash across the front lawn. Frankie and Neet crouched beneath one of the front windows and peered in. The window stood slightly open and on the other side of the pretty lace curtains was a perfectly turned out sitting room. Pink lampshades, pink settees, pink wallpaper. There was even a pink pussycat prowling across the plush pink carpet. Frankie felt slightly nauseous, as if he had swallowed a vat of strawberry ice-cream. Then he saw a sight that sent a chill through his veins. Perched in the middle of the sofa, like an ancient doll, was a white-haired old lady with a curious pink smile.

'That's her!' Frankie whispered.

'Who?' Neet replied, baffled.

'Marvella Brand.'

Marvella was a strange sight to behold. Her wizened features were framed by white ringleted hair and she was wearing a prim satin party dress. Frankie noticed that she was clutching something between her crumpled hands. It was a rather tired-looking fairy wand. Marvella's pale eyes were focused intently on Timmy, who was engulfed in a puffy armchair, scoffing what looked like a handful of marshmallows.

'How charming!' the old lady trilled, swinging her legs forward and clapping her hands together like a little girl. 'How simply delightful! You must come round to play more often!' Frankie winced. Like her famous permafrost smile, there was something chilly about Marvella's voice.

'Now,' said Marvella, 'what have you found out about our little party-poopers?'

'Can I have my vouchers?' said Timmy through a mouthful of mallow.

'No,' said Marvella with a sugary snap. 'Information first, vouchers later.' Timmy pulled a sulky face, but there was something about Marvella that you didn't want to trifle with.

'Well, Frankie hasn't brought his Mechanimal into school for a while . . .' Timmy began.

Frankie and Neet stared at each other. So they were right. Timmy *had* been following them. '. . . He doesn't seem to want to play with Mechanimals any more – which is weird – and Neet is always hanging out at his house with that mad old French lady, and then the other day I saw them snooping around the shop. Frankie went right into the grotto and—'

'That's enough!' hissed Marvella in a voice that sounded like an icicle snapping. 'I was warned about this.' Marvella poured herself a cup of raspberry tea and sat silently, collecting her thoughts. She looked like one of those old porcelain dolls that Frankie's cousin Amelia collected. The sort that you are not supposed to play with in case its head falls off.

'Can I have my vouchers now?' Timmy asked again.

'You must do me a teensy-weensy favour first,' Marvella replied, '*then* you can have as many vouchers as you like, OK?'

'Fine,' grumbled Timmy. 'What is it?'

'All I want you to do,' Marvella cooed, 'is bring your two little friends—'

'They're not my friends,' Timmy scoffed, through a sugary mouthful.

'Whatever,' snapped Marvella. 'Bring Frankie and Anita to the store tomorrow lunchtime. I need to get them out of the way for a while. We don't want them spoiling everybody's fun.' Frankie and Neet looked at each other in horror.

'But . . .' Timmy seemed suddenly uncomfortable. 'But what are you going to do to them?'

Marvella burst into a peal of silver laughter. 'Silly boy!' she said. 'We're not going to *do* anything to them. We just need to send them on a little trip, that's all. Like a holiday.'

'Well, I guess that's OK,' Timmy replied cautiously. 'And then I'll get my vouchers, right?'

'That's it!' Neet hissed through her teeth. 'I've had enough of this! I'm going in there right now! We need to know what's going on!'

'Shhh!' warned Frankie, catching her arm. His gut was telling him that the danger they were in was very real. 'Remember what Alphonsine said. We have to be patient.'

Neet muttered in annoyance but they stayed where they were, as still and as silent as snails.

Soon, Timmy was sent scurrying out of the

door. They were about to follow him back when Neet heard the beeps of a telephone being dialled. They peeked through the lace curtains and saw Marvella clutching a large pink receiver between her tiny hands. 'Is everything ready for the meeting tomorrow morning?' she hissed between her pearly white teeth. A voice at the other end of the line burbled a reply, but Frankie and Neet couldn't make out the words. 'No. No more time,' snapped Marvella. 'Christmas is just around the corner– we can't delay a moment longer. Besides, I have given you everything you need – the elves, the workshops. Now I expect to see results.'

'Who is she talking to?' said Neet. 'You don't think she's kidnapped Santa, do you?' Frankie was straining his ears to hear the other voice. Something had snagged in his brain, but he couldn't tell what it was.

'Yes, yes,' Marvella continued. 'They will both

be delivered tomorrow, as you requested. One of their classmates will be bringing them in; a greedy little goblin called Timmy . . . Yes, he'll be there. He'd bring his own granny if he thought there was a voucher in it.'

Frankie and Neet exchanged glances. Marvella was probably right about that.

The voice at the end of the line buzzed anxiously. 'Listen,' Marvella snapped. 'If it wasn't for me you'd still be scampering round your cage eating sunflower seeds.'

Frankie felt his stomach tighten.

'You should remember that I only put my time and money into rescuing you because I heard about your pioneering work with children. The Marvella Brand corporation has invested a great deal in *Project Wishlist*,' Marvella continued frostily, 'now we expect results.' The burbling at the other end of the line subsided. 'You are the world's top brain scientist,' she said. 'I don't expect to be disappointed.'

Suddenly, Frankie knew – with absolute certainty – who was on the other end of the line. He felt his skin shivering into hundreds of goosebumps.

'Goodnight, Dr Gore,' Marvella hissed through her stretched smile. 'Don't let the children down.'

Chapter Fifteen
The Break-in

'I should have known Dr Gore was behind all of this!' Eddie exclaimed, pacing back and forth across the kitchen. 'It's got his fingerprints all over it!'

'Well it would explain what happened to Snuffles,' said Neet. 'But how . . . how did they turn him back into a human being?'

'There's nothing very human about Dr Gore,' said Frankie and shuddered. Just saying his enemy's name was enough to send a shiver of dread down his spine.

'Marvella has an awful lot of money,' sighed Eddie. 'If she wants something done there is not a lot that will get in her way. This time she wanted Dr Gore's brainpower. She probably tracked him down and struck a deal: she would follow his instructions to turn him back into a human if he would promise to work for her. Simple as that.'

'Simple for an evil genius, yes,' muttered Alphonsine, sucking pensively on her coffee.

'But what do they want with us?' Neet stammered.

Alphonsine narrowed her two grey eyes. 'Something most evil is afoot in that emporium, no doubts about it,' she said, 'and Dr Gore doesn't want you two mangling it up for him like last time. That's why he needs to get you out of the way.'

Neet stamped her foot in frustration. 'We're

running out of time,' she said. '*Project Wishlist* is already underway but we don't have the first idea how to stop it. We don't even know what happened to Wes!'

Frankie nodded. Neet was right. They hadn't even started to join the dots. There was the mind-sweeping, the morse code, the message. But what did it all add up to?

'Marvella said something about a meeting,' said Frankie. 'We need to find a way in.' Everyone nodded in agreement. 'It is being held tomorrow morning, so I say we break into Marvella's tonight.'

'Sure,' said Neet, 'but how? It's a fortress. The whole place is alarmed. There are cameras everywhere. They'll catch us in a flash and hand us over to Dr Gore!' Frankie felt a panic rising in his chest as he remembered the time Dr Gore had locked him in a dark cupboard until he thought he'd go mad with fear. But Alphonsine seemed strangely calm. She reached into her apron pocket and pulled out a large, grubby-looking piece of paper. 'Look what I found in ze dustbin!' she grinned. Alphonsine spread the paper out on the table and sat back triumphantly. It was the architect's plans for Marvella's store.

'What did I tell you?' smiled Eddie proudly. 'Nobody knows how to rummage in a bin like my Alfie!'

The friends stayed up till the early hours of the morning plotting their break-in. Neet was right. It was a fortress. All the doors were heavily bolted and alarmed, and there were security cameras all the way around the building. But there was one route in – via a small air vent at the side of the shop. It looked just about wide enough for Neet and Frankie to crawl through, but there was no way Alfie or Eddie could come with them.

After Alphonsine had removed the vent-cover with her trusty screwdriver Frankie and Neet would be on their own.

It was three in the morning by the time Alphonsine's motorbike purred to a halt outside Marvella's. The store looked quite different at night. In the early-morning gloom, it looked less like a fairytale castle and more like an enormous black dragon. The towers and turrets ended in menacing spikes that pierced the sky and the cold light of the moon drained the rosy cheeks of the toy soldiers. Frankie felt a shudder pass through his ribcage.

'Good luck, little cabbages,' said Alphonsine. She unfixed the vent-cover then gave Frankie a leg up.

Frankie flashed his torch into the vent shaft and gulped. The tunnel was full of cobwebs and incredibly narrow. Once you were in, there was no turning around and if you got stuck . . . well, Frankie tried not to think about it. The two friends helped each other clamber in, then they crawled and squeezed their way through, inch by inch, until they eventually dropped out into the shop.

'Urrrgh, this place gives me the creeps,' Neet whispered as they dusted themselves down and flicked off the fat little spiders they had picked up along the way.

Frankie swung the torchlight about him. Without the music and the movement of mechanical toys, the shop felt as desolate as an empty fairground. Puppets hung twisted in the air and animal masks grimaced at them through the darkness.

'Let's get a move on, Frankie,' Neet whispered urgently. 'I can't shake the feeling that we're being watched.'

Frankie had exactly the same feeling. Perhaps it was the hard, shiny eyes of all those stuffed animals. He wasn't sure. He picked up a teddy bear and looked at it closely. 'I think you're right, Neet,' he whispered. 'Look at this.' Buried in the bear's eye-sockets were two tiny security cameras with blinking red centres. 'There are cameras everywhere. Grab those masks.'

Neet took a plastic tiger mask and Frankie slipped on a grinning monkey face. Then they stealthily made their way to the staff door at the back of the shop and climbed the stairs up to Marvella's headquarters.

'Brrr,' shuddered Neet as they entered the slick glass corridors of Marvella's business empire. 'It's chilly in here.' The playful paraphernalia of the toyshop had disappeared and in its place were the hard lines and grey carpets of a modern office.

'This is where Marvella's employees work,'

said Frankie, spotting the diagram of the child's brain that he had seen from the fire escape.

Suddenly, the beam of Frankie's torch flashed across a vision that made him shriek with fright. Looming over him was an enormous furry face with two black holes for eyes.

'WAAAAAGH!' screamed Frankie, dropping his torch and scrambling for the door.

'Hang on a minute! Hang on, Frankie!' Neet called, casting the torch back towards the source of Frankie's terror. 'Wait! It's just Teddy Manywishes, look!'

Frankie looked. Teddy Manywishes' costume was hanging up on the coatstand, sagging and empty like an enormous chrysalis. Frankie felt quite shaken. But there was no time to waste.

'Come on, Frankie,' said Neet, 'let's get cracking! There's got to be something here.'

Neet and Frankie started to dredge through

the paperwork that littered the desks and spilt out of filing cabinets. The store may have been selling toys, but there was nothing amusing about the business that went on there. Frankie yawned as he sifted through stacks of legal documents, graphs and calculations. It was like the worst kind of homework ever.

'I don't understand any of this!' he grumbled.

'I know, I know,' said Neet, who was just as befuddled as Frankie, 'and the sun's coming up, look! We're running out of time!' But then, amongst all the papers and calculations and pie-charts, Frankie's eye alighted on a name.

Wesley Archibald Vernon Jones.

It was near the top of a long list of names that looked rather like a school register.

'Neet! Neety!' cried Frankie. 'It's Wes's name, look!'

'Wow, Frankie, you're right,' gasped Neet,

studying the list. 'There couldn't be another Wesley Archibald Vernon Jones, could there?'

'I doubt it!' said Frankie. 'But why would they have his name?'

Neet read the words at the top of the list out loud: '*The Elves*'.

Frankie's heart skipped a beat as he remembered those grinning waxen faces in the grotto.

'Who *are* the elves?' Neet wondered.

'I thought Wes was staying with his Auntie Elv . . .' Neet paused before she got to the end of the word.

Frankie looked her straight in the eye. 'There isn't an Auntie Elvira, is there?'

There was a creak and rumble of an elevator in motion. The two friends jumped out of their skins. Somebody was in the building! Frankie ran to the window. The sun was rising in the sky and

Marvella's employees were beginning to arrive for work.

'Quickly!' Frankie whispered in terror as they hurriedly stuffed the papers back into their files. They heard the march of footsteps down the corridor. They were trapped.

Frankie looked frantically about him. There was a door at the side of the room. 'This way!' whispered Frankie, pulling Neet towards it and praying it was unlocked. They were in luck. Frankie and Neet crashed through the door and slammed it behind them, panting with fear.

Looking about, they found themselves in a large auditorium that must have been able to hold a couple of hundred people. Frankie scanned the room for a hiding place. Against the wall stood a drinks trolley covered loosely with a white tablecloth. They both squeezed themselves under the trolley and pulled down the cloth.

'What do we do now, Frankie?' Neet gulped.

They could hear the low chatter and the whirring of computers starting up as people arrived for work. Frankie peeked through a small gap in the tablecloth. At the front of the auditorium, behind the stage was a large screen, and on it, in swirly pink letters, were the words: '*Project Wishlist*'.

Frankie took a deep breath.

'We wait.'

Chapter Sixteen
The Meeting

Frankie and Neet waited. And they waited. They stayed cramped under the trolley for so long that Frankie felt as if his body had been squashed into a cube like a lump of scrap metal. Then, just when he thought he might actually rust, there was a loud chatter of voices and the doors swung open. People were beginning to arrive for the meeting.

Frankie squinted through the gap in the cloth. Men and women in suits and slick hair were filing into the room and finding seats. There was a buzz in the air and the odd burst of hearty laughter shook the room.

'I heard they cracked it,' one lady drawled through a thin pair of lips. Frankie recognised her as the woman with the tight bun that he had seen through the window of Marvella's the week before. 'Looks like we're in the money.' The man she was speaking to guffawed and smoothed the lapels of his jacket.

'I should hope so,' he sneered. 'We've thrown enough cash at it.' The woman narrowed her eyes and turned down the corners of her mouth.

'Marvella may look crazy,' she replied, 'but she's as sharp as they come – you'll see. Drink?' Frankie and Neet held their breath as the woman stepped towards the trolley and poured a glass of water. Her shoes were as black and shiny as an oil slick and the toe was so sharply pointed it made Frankie pull back in alarm.

'Who are these people?' Frankie whispered.

'Investors,' said Neet, proud that she knew such a grown-up word. 'They're the people paying for all this. If Marvella sells a lot of toys, then they will make a lot of money.'

'How do you know all that?' asked Frankie, impressed.

'Some of us actually listen in class, you know.' Neet smiled, giving him a pinch on the arm.

Suddenly the lights dimmed and the Marvella theme tune jingled over the speakers. Everybody hushed. Frankie peered through the gap in the cloth. Standing in the middle of the stage like a tiny Christmas fairy was the big boss of the global toy trade, the queen of games and gadgets, the high priestess of presents – Marvella Brand.

Marvella may have been no bigger than a garden gnome, but her porcelain stillness commanded absolute attention. She smiled pinkly at the audience as if she were contemplating an enormous box of chocolates and began.

'Welcome,' she tinkled, clasping her small white hands in front of her satin party dress. 'Welcome to my marvellous toyshop, my fabulous kingdom where children's dreams come true!' The audience was as entranced as toddlers at a magic show. 'We have some special treats in store for you today,' Marvella continued, her smile spreading like strawberry jam, 'so let's begin!'

Marvella clapped her hands and the room was instantly filled with the sound of sleigh-bells. Frankie and Neet peered out carefully from behind the tablecloth so that they could get a better view. The screen was flickering to life and showing a series of happy Christmas scenes: fir trees twinkled, rosy-cheeked children unwrapped presents, and happy parents beamed with joy.

Then a thick, treacly voice like the ones you hear in adverts began to speak over the music.

'We all know that Christmas is a special time of year,' it oozed. *'It is a special time for children and for their mummies and daddies. But most of all it is a special time for toyshops.'*

Frankie frowned. That didn't sound right. The images changed to show a large wobbly graph with lots of dollar signs that Frankie could make no sense of whatsoever.

The voice continued, *'Christmas is not only a time for caring and sharing, it is also a time for spending. This Christmas, the Marvella Corporation is set to take the largest slice of the Christmas pudding. With your support, our team of experts has been working hard on "Project Wishlist" – a revolutionary way to make sure that Marvella's toys are the only thing on children's minds, this year, next year and every year to come. Yes indeed, the future is Marvella's and the cash registers will be ringing, ringing, ringing out for Christmas!'*

A smiling Teddy Manywishes flashed up on to the screen. Frankie felt ill.

'*Marvella Brand's Happyland,*' said the treacly voice. '*We know what children want.*'

The audience stroked their chins in thought. They were impressed.

Marvella trotted back to the centre of the stage, as if she were about to perform a tap-dance.

'At Marvella's,' she said, placing her hands on her heart, 'we are devoted to children's happiness. We never stop asking ourselves: What are the little darlings thinking? What they are dreaming about? What lights up their little eyes and makes their hearts go *boom*?' Marvella's smile broke into a shower of tinkling laughter. 'In fact,' she continued, 'we are so committed to making children's dreams come true that we have tracked down one of the top brains in the world to make it all happen.'

Frankie felt a shiver run down his spine as if somebody had dropped a dead fish down the back of his shirt. He knew what was coming next.

'Will you please welcome the brains behind *Project Wishlist,* the gentleman whose tireless work and dedication to children has made all this possible. Move over Santa Claus. Make way for Dr Calus Gore!'

CHAPTER SEVENTEEN
THE EXPLORER

Frankie couldn't believe what he was seeing. Dr Calus Gore who, not so long ago, had been scurrying round a hamster wheel in 4D's classroom was now striding on to the stage, grinning like an imp. He looked just the same as he did when he was headmaster of Crammar Grammar, only instead of his headmasterly robes he wore the sort of long white coat that doctors wear when they are about to stick a needle in your arm. The scientist's yellowish eyes ranged over the room and his curled moustache twitched like a large black moth. Frankie frowned. No, he didn't look *exactly* the same. There was something changed about him. Frankie couldn't put a finger on what it was – until he opened his mouth to speak.

'Thank you, thank you,' he smirked. 'Thank you, Marvella, for your most accurate introduction.'

Frankie had to suppress a giggle. Rather than the grating tone of his headmaster days, Gore's voice kept veering into high-pitched squeaks. Whatever scientific wizardry Dr Gore had used to transform himself back into a person had not been completely successful. Dr Gore was *still* part rat. His front teeth were long and pointy and Frankie could have sworn that his ears were bigger and tuftier.

'He sounds just like Teddy Manywishes!' Neet whispered. Frankie did a double-take.

'Wow, you're right!' he replied. 'He *is* Teddy Manywishes. It must have been him in that costume when he came to visit the school!' Frankie shivered to think that his old enemy had been so close and he hadn't even known it.

Dr Gore pressed the tips of his bony fingers together as he waited for the audience to settle.

'Ladies and gentlemen,' he began, jutting his chin in the air, 'I like to think of myself as an explorer!'

Oh here we go! thought Frankie, sensing that Dr Gore was about to launch into one of his lectures. *We'll be stuck here for ages.*

The scientist sucked a lungful of air slowly through his narrow nostrils. '. . . An explorer of the mind.' He paused for dramatic effect. 'The mind of the child is a ghastly place,' he continued. 'I know. I have seen it. Children may look like harmless little gnomes, but believe me, there are sinister things lurking inside those tiny heads.'

There was a splutter of nervous laughter. Who was this strange fellow?

'Beneath those blond curls,' Dr Gore went on,

'between those pink ears, is a primitive jungle full of hidden dangers and creeping with monsters!'

'What is he on about?' said Neet.

'Search me,' said Frankie. 'I never understand a word he says.'

'Who here has read a child's story or seen a child's drawing?' asked Dr Gore, lifting two bristling eyebrows. A number of hands went up. 'Well then, you will know that a child's mind is full of the most abysmal nonsense. Fairy stories, magic, clowns, talking animals – children have no sense of reality whatsoever!' Dr Gore's moustache was twitching so fast Frankie thought it might fly off and flutter round the room like a bat. 'But I, Dr Calus Gore, have fearlessly ventured into this wilderness and I shall tell you what I saw.'

The audience shifted in their seats, intrigued by the weird brilliance of the speaker.

The scientist flicked on the video projector

and a large picture of a child's brain appeared on the screen. It was divided into different colour-coded areas and at the centre was a large dark spot. 'As you can see,' Gore sniffed, 'the child's brain has only a few basic functions. This part . . .' Gore tapped the green area with his fingernail, '. . . is for problem-solving. Children mostly use it for pointless activities like jigsaw puzzles.' He gave a snort of contempt. 'The pink area here,' he continued, 'is for inventing things or, in other words, making up the most appalling drivel. You would not believe the ludicrous creations I have encountered there: green horses, talking toothbrushes, flying monkeys in bowler hats!'

The audience laughed, but Dr Gore did not see the funny side.

Widening his yellow eyes, Gore pointed to the mysterious dark zone at the centre of the diagram. 'But it is here . . .' he said in hushed tones, 'that I

have discovered the deepest, darkest possibilities of the child's mind. This is the part of the mind that makes the child the person they are. It is the *core*, the keystone, the smouldering volcano at the centre of the island. It is where we find their most secret thoughts, their most intense feelings and their most precious memories. It is *this* that we must colonise if we are to win the race to Christmas!' Dr Gore was so worked up that Frankie thought he could see a plume of steam rising from the dome of his head.

The audience muttered amongst themselves. They weren't yet sure what to make of this odd chap and his even odder ideas. 'I'm not sure where he's going with this,' whispered one.

'I hope Marvella knows what she's doing,' muttered another, 'or it'll cost us.'

Then a silver-haired man who had been huffing and puffing for the past few minutes lost his patience and thrust his hand into the air. 'This is all well and good, Professor,' he began, in a voice that sounded like the stomping of boots, 'but what we want to know is how all this is going to pay off. How is it going to make us money?'

There was a general nodding of heads.

'I believe Dr Gore is just getting to that.' Marvella smiled frostily. 'Aren't you, Dr Gore?'

Dr Gore grimaced and narrowed his eyes. He could see that he was surrounded by idiots. 'Of course,' he hissed through his enormous front teeth. 'The first stage of *Project Wishlist* is complete. We have extracted the mind-matter from the core of children's brains and stored it on a database.'

'That's what the Mechanimals are for,' whispered Frankie, remembering his own memory flashing on to the screen in Marvella's creepy computer lab. 'They've been robbing our brains and beaming our thoughts back here.'

But the man who asked the question wasn't satisfied.

'So what did you find out?' he puffed. 'What *do* children want?'

Dr Gore rolled his eyes. 'My dear ssssir,' he hissed, 'you are asking the wrong question. Children, as we all know well, do not want *anything* for very long. One day it's a toy castle, the next it's a spaceship, the day after that it's a pirate costume. Today, they all want Mechanimals but next week it will be something else entirely. All this makes life very difficult for toyshops.' The audience nodded in agreement – he was spot on there. Dr Gore smiled his piranha smile. 'So I have sssimplified things. The purpose of *Project Wishlist* is not to *find out* what children want, but to *tell* them what they want.'

'How do you propose to do that?' the gentleman sniffed.

'Sssimple,' hissed Dr Gore, spreading his

fingers like a magician. 'Advertising.' Dr Gore's grin twinkled in the spotlight.

'Advertising?' scoffed the gentleman. 'But that's the oldest trick in the book!'

'You misunderstand, dear sir,' Dr Gore continued. 'This won't be any old advertising. It won't be the sort that you watch as you're eating your cornflakes and forget by the time you've brushed your teeth. No! This kind of advertising will go straight to the core of the child's mind and lodge itself there for eternity. Think of it as upgrading their brains, giving their minds a makeover.'

'What do you mean?' asked the woman with the pointy shoes.

'As we speak,' said Dr Gore, 'there is a team of computing experts working on the memories that we have harvested from children's brains up and down the country. Into this mind-matter they are inserting Marvella logos, Marvella products and the Marvella jingle. Let me demonstrate.' Dr Gore pushed a button and the screen lit up. 'This memory belongs to little Viola Fordham of Oxford, England.' The screen showed a little girl playing cricket with her mum on the beach. 'The sun is shining, the sea is sparkling, the ice-cream is melting. It is a perfect day, is it not? It is a memory that Viola will no doubt cherish for years to come. But our laboratory has added some finishing touches. I shall now give you the new and improved version of little Viola's memory. See if you can spot the difference!'

Dr Gore restarted the film. The exact same memory replayed, only this time there were two striking differences. Firstly, Viola's mother was wearing a T-shirt with a large Marvella logo on it and secondly the ice-cream van in the distance was playing the Marvella jingle over and over and over again. Dr Gore had turned Viola's memory into an advert for Marvella Brand's Happyland. The audience oohed and aahed in astonishment. This was extraordinary! Revolutionary! The man was a genius, no doubt about it. Dr Gore puffed up like an adder.

'At midnight tonight,' he continued, 'when little Viola is tucked up in bed dreaming of dancing sugarplums and other such nonsense, the Mechanimals will switch her old memories for these new, improved versions. All Viola's warm, fuzzy feelings about family holidays, her mummy, the seaside and so on, shall be instantly transferred on to our toys. And the results shall be astounding. From tomorrow morning,' Gore shouted triumphantly, 'whenever children see the Marvella logo or hear the Marvella tune they will become convinced that owning our toys is the very key to happiness. At the same time, they will feel certain that – should they fail to own them – they will be as worthless as dung-beetles.

In short, they will be overcome by an irresistible desire for as many Marvella toys as they can get their sticky little fingers on. Not just this Christmas, not just next Christmas, but every day till the end of their childhoods!'

The audience exploded into waves of applause. They were impressed, very impressed.

'He wants to turn us into drones!' whispered Neet, appalled. 'It's horrible! Horrible! I can't believe he's been poking around inside my head!'

'It's OK, Neet,' Frankie said, trying to sound much braver than he felt. 'We'll stop him. We'll find a way.'

All of a sudden there was a faint knock at the door, just next to where Neet and Frankie were hiding.

'Hello?' said a small, nervous voice.

It was Timmy.

CHAPTER EIGHTEEN
THE TRACKER

'A five-minute break, my good people,' Dr Gore grinned, spotting Timmy peeking round the door. 'I have something urgent to see to.' Gore and Marvella both headed towards Timmy as the audience chattered excitedly amongst themselves.

'Well?' smiled Marvella, in a voice that sounded like the squeak of snow underfoot.

'Ummm . . . errrr . . . the thing is . . .' Timmy fumbled. Frankie felt the air temperature drop as Marvella's patience thinned like ice on a lake.

'They didn't come into school today,' blurted Timmy. 'It wasn't my fault, Miss.'

Dr Gore's eyes bulged out of his head like a rat caught in a trap. 'So where *are* they?' he spat. 'We must find them. We must root them out!'

'It's not my fault, sir,' Timmy whined. 'That's all I came to say. Can I have my vouchers now?'

'No you can't have—' spluttered Dr Gore, the veins on his head pulsing like earthworms.

Marvella interrupted. 'Don't you listen to that mean old man, Timmy dear,' she soothed. 'Rudolph, my secretary, will give you as many vouchers as you can stuff in your pockets.'

'Uh, OK . . . thanks!' stammered Timmy. Marvella clicked her fingers and Frankie heard the thud of heavy feet advancing down the corridor.

'You're welcome,' Marvella smiled. Moments later there was the sound of a scuffle.

'Ow! Let go!' Timmy shrieked. 'Get off! What are you doing?' Marvella closed the door as Timmy was dragged away down the corridor. 'Where are you taking me?! Heeeelp!' he yelled. Frankie and Neet exchanged alarmed glances. The door clicked shut.

Dr Gore was white with fury. 'You told me they'd be here!' he spluttered. 'We must find them IMMEDIATELY!'

'I don't see why you're throwing such a tantrum,' Marvella tutted. 'So what if we don't find them? It's too late for them to stop us now.'

'Oh-ho!' Dr Gore spluttered through his moustache. 'You don't know what the little vandals are capable of! Frankie Blewitt and Anita Banerjee are vicious little crooks, I tell you, criminal masterminds!'

'Calm yourself!' Marvella hissed slowly, like a snapping icicle. 'People are staring. Now you have a job to do, so slap on a smile, get up there and get on with it!'

Marvella's orders were as clear as crystal. Dr Gore mopped his enormous forehead, ratcheted up a tense grin and returned to the admiring crowd.

'This is all very impressive, Professor,' ventured a man with a wispy moustache. 'But . . . um . . . is it entirely ethical? I mean, it all seems a little . . . extreme, don't you think?' The audience murmured uncomfortably while Dr Gore's yellow eyes flared with contempt.

'My dear ssssir,' he sneered, 'scientific progress demands—' But Marvella didn't let him get any further.

'At Marvella's,' she piped up shrilly, 'we will go to great lengths to give children what they want for Christmas. We are extreme, yes, and I'm not afraid to say it. Extremely committed to children's happiness, and . . .' she added with a wink, 'extremely committed to your bank balance.' The audience chuckled and did not press any further. After all, why stand in the way of progress? Why stand in the way of children's happiness?

'One more thing,' Gore hissed. 'To make sure everything goes to plan, we are keeping the children under tight surveillance. Last week we targeted a test-group from the local school.' The screen flicked on to show security camera footage of the Cramley children on their visit to the toyshop.

'Good grief,' gasped Frankie. 'That's you, Neet, look. And there's Esther, and Jasmine, and Benny.'

Dr Gore wrinkled his nose with displeasure and continued.

'Each of these children was given a tracking device, so that we can keep an eye on their movements. We want to know their migration patterns. Do they travel in groups, or on their own? How fast do they move past shop windows? And so on.'

'I don't remember getting a tracking device,' said Neet. 'I don't get it.'

The projection screen flicked on to show a bird's-eye view of the town with several dozen small red dots moving around it.

'Each dot,' crowed Dr Gore, 'represents a child of Cramley school and . . .'

'Wow!' whispered Neet, dazzled by the technical wizardry. 'That's pretty cool!'

'No, Neet,' said Frankie, turning pale. Dr Gore had halted mid-sentence and was glaring silently at a spot on the map. Frankie thought he could hear the scientist's blood beginning to simmer. 'Empty your pockets, Neet!' whispered Frankie urgently.

Neet did as Frankie said and – along with a

few hairy toffees and a crusty old hankie – an *I Love Marvella's* badge came tumbling out.

'That's it, Neet!' Frankie panicked. 'That's the tracking device! The badge!' Frankie peeped through the spyhole and saw Dr Gore striding off the stage towards them, his long fingers twitching like angry spiders. 'He knows we're here!'

Chapter Nineteen
The Hideaway

The audience gasped as two children in animal masks shot out from under the drinks trolley, dived through Dr Gore's legs and flew out of the room faster than a pair of rocket-propelled rollerskates.

'Bleeeeewiiiiit!!! Baaaaanerjeeeeeeeee!!!!' the scientist shrieked in his chipmunky voice. 'Get back here!!' But Frankie and Neet were doing no such thing. They tore down the stairs as fast as their legs would carry them. Frankie was breathing so hard he thought his lungs would burst into flames. But he couldn't slow down for a second. He knew what Dr Calus Gore was capable of and he wasn't about to take any chances. Alarms wailed and flashed all around them. Marvella had alerted security. Frankie glanced over his shoulder to see two enormous security guards charging after them like angry rhinos.

'Come in, Blitzen! Come in, Blitzen!' one of them honked into his walkie-talkie. 'We have located the party-poopers. Repeat. We have located the party-poopers.'

'Read that, Donner,' a voice crackled back. 'I've got the exits covered.'

Frankie and Neet exchanged panicked glances. 'This way, Frankie,' said Neet, pushing through a side door that led straight into the shop. The store was already heaving with shoppers. Frankie and Neet pushed into the throng, but the guards were catching up fast. Frankie turned his head to see one of them right behind him, reaching forwards with a huge, hairy hand.

'The smoke-bomb!' Frankie cried. 'Quickly!'

Neet pulled the perfume bottle out of her pocket and yanked the chain. *Whooooooooooosh!* Within moments the shop was filled with a thick blue fog, so dense that Frankie couldn't even see his own feet.

'We're getting out of here, Frankie,' called Neet. 'Hold on to my ponytail.' The crowd began to shout and shove their way towards the exit. Frankie felt himself being carried along on a surge of people that was so thick and fast-moving he was afraid he might drown. 'Hold on, Frankie!' called Neet. Frankie took a deep breath, then, before he knew it, he tumbled out of the fog and crush of the shop into the crisp winter air.

'Nice one, Neet!' said Frankie coughing the

smoke from his lungs. 'Now we need to get home and tell the others.'

But Neet didn't reply.

'Neet?'

Frankie felt an enormous hand clamp down on the back of his neck and winch him off his feet. It was Rudolph, the henchman that had taken Timmy away. Frankie saw that Neet was in his other hand, wiggling and squeaking like a gerbil. The guard turned them both around to face him and grinned like an enormous toddler playing with glove-puppets. Frankie tried to shout but Rudolph's huge thumb was squeezing his throat so tightly, he could only draw the thinnest wisp of air into his lungs. He felt the sweat beading on his forehead and saw stars floating before his eyes. Then, just as he was about to black out, he heard a shrill howl of pain. The guard's enormous fists sprang open, dropping Neet and Frankie on to the pavement. 'Waaaaaaah!' yelled Rudolph clutching, his bottom. 'Owweeeeee!' Frankie couldn't work out what had happened. But then he heard the most ferocious barking. So savage were the growls he felt sure a wolf had escaped from the zoo. But no! Frankie recognised those fluffy white ears and that pink satin collar. Colette! The poodle let go of the guard's trousers and, as he went howling back into the shop, she trotted delicately over to Frankie and licked the tip of his nose.

'Thanks, Colette!' gasped Frankie, catching his breath. 'You're a lifesaver!'

The familiar sound of a motorbike engine revved behind them.

'Let's go, little cabbages!' cried Alphonsine, chucking them a helmet each. 'No time to be fandangling about!'

Neet and Frankie swung themselves on to Alphonsine's growling panther of a bike and within minutes they were roaring away from the toyshop and out of town. As they sped into the countryside, they told Alphonsine about everything they had discovered at Marvella's. By the time they had finished, Alphonsine was crosser than a plateful of hot-cross buns.

'Disgracious!' she fumed. 'Disgustful! Snitching children's memories and turning zem into adverts! That Dr Calus is as mad as a mushroom!' Colette growled in agreement. 'We must stop him! Straightaway! Once and forever!

The motorbike turned off the main road on to a muddy path that led into the forest.

'Where are we going, Alfie?' Frankie hollered over the engine.

'We can't go home,' Alphonsine yelled back. 'Somebody has been there. Somebody has turned the place outside-in.'

'What do you mean?' Neet shouted.

'When Eddie got back, somebody had broken into the house,' she shouted. 'One of Gore's little spies no doubt, sniffling around, trying to find you. It is not safe. I am taking you to a tip-top secret hideaway. We is meeting Eddie there.'

Neet and Frankie clung on tightly as Alphonsine's motorbike lurched valiantly over muddy ditches and around clumps of twisted roots. The forest was so densely tangled that, within minutes, Frankie felt completely lost. But Alphonsine's sense of direction was as sensitive as a bloodhound's nostril and, before long, they were nearing their destination.

Wiping the mud from his visor, Frankie glimpsed a distant bloom of colour through the trees. The motorbike's tyres churned on up a narrow, winding path and, little by little, a tall, rickety cabin came into view.

'Ooooh!' cooed Neet. The cabin was as

colourful as a gypsy caravan. Huge petals of paint were peeling off the wooden walls and swallows flitted in and out of the holes in the sloping roof as if they were weaving it together with threads of air. It was clear that nobody had set foot there for a very long time, but it had a certain magic that hadn't faded.

'Where are we?' asked Frankie. Alphonsine put her finger to her lips and approached the cabin, eyes flicking from side to side to check they had not been followed. Then, *toc-a-toc-toc*, she rapped swiftly on the bright blue door.

As Eddie opened up, Frankie's eyes widened in astonishment. He stepped inside and looked around him. The dusty rays of light that streamed through the broken roof illuminated the most extraordinary collection of objects Frankie had ever seen. Draped with a layer of silky cobwebs were miniature merry-go-rounds and wind-up dragons, clockwork unicorns and mechanical mermaids. He felt like a giant who had accidentally wandered into a fairytale kingdom, frozen in time. Frankie approached what looked like a workbench. On its surface was a pair of dusty old spectacles and a log-book embossed with two deep-set letters. Frankie rubbed the dust away with his thumb to reveal two small, golden initials. *C.W.*

Eddie nodded and told Frankie what he already knew.

'A very long time ago,' he said, 'this was Crispin Whittle's workshop.'

Chapter Twenty
The Clock

'Do you think we're safe here?' asked Frankie.

'Perfectly,' Eddie replied. 'Marvella is the only other person who knows about this place, but she never visits.'

'Are you sure?' whispered Neet, nervously.

Eddie nodded. 'After her uncle died, many moons ago, she never returned. Too many sad memories, I suppose.'

Frankie picked up a tarnished picture frame and gave it a wipe. In it was a yellowing photograph of a sprightly-looking fellow with round glasses and tufts of hair sprouting from his ears. A little girl sat daintily on his lap. She had sparkling eyes and an eager smile that seemed to warm the glass of the frame.

'That's her,' said Eddie.

'Really?' Frankie replied, struggling to believe it. 'You wouldn't know it, would you?'

'Hey look at this,' said Neet, picking up a large cream-coloured envelope. The envelope had been lying on the bench for so many years it left a dark oblong shadow in the dust. 'It's addressed to Marvella. It must be from her uncle.'

'Let's have a look,' said Frankie, taking the envelope and turning it between his fingers. He was about to open it when Eddie swiped it out of his hands.

'Manners!' said Eddie, tweaking Frankie's ear affectionately. 'Don't you know it's rude to read other people's mail?'

‘Sorry, Eddie.’ Frankie blushed.

‘I’ll make sure it gets to its owner,’ Eddie replied, dusting it off and slipping it into his pocket, ‘Better late than never.’

Alphonsine made up a fire in the ash-filled hearth and, as they huddled round the greenish flames, they plotted their next move. There was no time to lose. Come midnight, *Project Wishlist* would launch into action. In bedrooms all over the country Mechanimals would be crawling out of their toy boxes, clambering on to their sleeping owners and giving their minds a full Marvella makeover.

‘We *have* to find a way to sabotage *Project Wishlist*,’ said Frankie. ‘All those logos and jingles need to be deleted before the Mechanimals put them into children’s heads.’

Everyone nodded in agreement. Yes indeed, that was what had to be done. But who would do it? Who *could* do it? Alphonsine was a spectacular mechanic. She could fix a motorbike or rewire a radio in no time at all, but neither she nor Eddie knew the first thing about computers.

'Ah!' sighed Alphonsine, shaking her head in frustration. 'I know nussing about these wizzy wotsits. Nussing at all. We never had ze chance to learn these things. We is too old, Frankie.'

Frankie and Neet looked at each other in dismay. They had computer classes once a week, but neither of them was very talented. Neet got decent scores on *Space Invaders*, but that wasn't the same as knowing how to program a computer. The technology that Dr Gore was using to transform children's memories was extremely complicated. Only an expert, a genius in fact, would be able to hack into Gore's systems and reverse all the damage being done.

'We need Wes!' Neet cried, stamping her foot in

frustration. Wes was a total whizz with computers. There was nothing he didn't know about gigabytes, cookies, firewalls, widgets and dongles. Frankie's head hurt just thinking about what all those words might mean, but Wes was a fearless cyber-explorer. No computer program could outsmart him. But where *was* Wes?

Suddenly, Frankie had a brainwave.

'Do you still have that Christmas card, Neet?' he asked. 'The one Wes sent us.' Neet dug into her pocket and handed it to Frankie.

'It's not much use.' She shrugged. 'There's no return address.'

'I know,' said Frankie. 'But what if he is trying to tell us something? Look . . .' Frankie pointed to the picture on the front of the card. It showed Santa Claus and his elves loading up the sleigh.

'Elves!' Neet exclaimed. 'Like that list we found in the office. The one with Wes's name on it.'

'Exactly.' Frankie opened the card and reread Wes's message. It was full of boring chit-chat about the weather – not like Wes at all.

'And all this stuff about the rain,' said Frankie. 'Maybe he's writing in code or something. He might be trying to tell us where he is.'

Eddie sat up in his chair and pointed at the card. 'If that's a code,' he said, 'then my Alphonsine will crack it. She'll crack a code faster than you can crack an egg, isn't that right, Alfie?' Alphonsine blushed a deep shade of crimson, but she didn't deny it.

Everyone held their breath as Alphonsine swivelled her glass eye firmly into place and set to work on Wes's message. She turned the letters this way and that, she read it backwards in the mirror, she applied complicated mathematical formulae and covered sheet upon sheet of paper with elaborate diagrams. But, as the minutes slipped by, she didn't seem to be making progress.

'Ach!' she puffed. 'I have never seen such a brain-bender!'

'A brain-teaser,' Eddie corrected her.

'Yes, yes,' muttered Alphonsine. 'Mind-teaser, brain-bender – my head is as scrambled as a breakfast!'

Frankie cast a worried glance at the old cuckoo clock above the fireplace – it was already past six. They all set their minds to the task. Neet got Frankie to read it out backwards, Eddie pretended it was a big crossword puzzle, and Colette sniffed at the letters with a frown of deep concentration, but not one of them could extract any sense from Wes's words. The sun had set hours ago and the team was getting desperate. The piles of screwed-up paper were mounting higher and higher, until all of a sudden . . .

Cuckoo! Midnight struck. Colette lifted her snout in the air and howled. They were too late.

CHAPTER TWENTY-ONE
MARVELLA-MANIA

The next morning the nation's children woke up feeling ever so slightly out of sorts. They had a strange swilling feeling in their bellies and felt as if their heads had been stuffed with cotton-wool. After a few fuzzy moments, they rubbed the sleep from their eyes, shuffled off to the bathroom to brush their teeth and started to feel normal again. However, there was nothing in the least bit normal about that particular December morning. Nothing normal at all.

At first, the children went about their usual

business. They ate their Weetabix, trudged off to school, giggled at a cheeky drawing of the teacher and swapped stickers. But before too long, the inevitable occurred. For some it happened when they were watching telly. For others it happened while they were listening to the radio, or staring out of the car window on their way to football practice. But, one way or the other, it happened. Sooner or later, every child in the country stumbled across an advertisment for Marvella Brand's Happyland and, at that moment, it was if an enormous Christmas cracker went off inside their brains.

Let me tell you what it felt like. Think about how you feel when you are starving hungry. Your belly starts to rumble, you can't think of anything else and you keep on moaning at your mum and dad until dinner is on the table. Well it was just like that, only children weren't desperate to be fed, they were desperate to get to the toyshop. As soon as a child saw a Marvella poster on a billboard, or heard Teddy Manywishes sing the Marvella song, they were gripped by an urgent desire for toys, toys and more toys. Not any old toys, mind you. It had to be Marvella toys – and right that very instant! There was no wrapping of presents or putting them under the tree or waiting till Christmas Day. No. The children had to have toys immediately and they were doing everything in their power to get them. From the peaks of the Scottish highlands to the shores of the Cornish coast a single cry could be heard, 'Muuuuuuum! Daaaaaaaad! Pleeeeeeeease!'

The grown-ups of the land couldn't work out what had happened. They had never known a craze like it. In fact it was far too crazy for a craze. The nation's children had gone completely and utterly bonkers. Teachers couldn't get them to sit still in lessons, babysitters couldn't get them to bed, and parents looked on in despair as their children screeched and squawked like hungry chicks. They were no longer interested in books, or football, or dance classes. They didn't talk about their friends or films or the big match on Saturday. All they thought about was Marvella Brand's Happyland. It was as if their whole world had shrunk to one long tunnel with a pair of golden doors at the end of it.

Right across the country, Marvella stores witnessed the most extraordinary scenes. So many children were hammering and howling at their windows that the shops were opening hours before time, and the moment the doors gave way, there was complete and utter pandemonium. Children stampeded into the shop like a herd of raging buffalo, then charged round the store seizing everything in sight. And hot on the heels of every child was an anxious parent wondering how they could possibly afford to buy everything their little angel was demanding. Within minutes, rows had broken out across the land. Children were sobbing, wailing and stamping their feet, parents were digging to the bottom of their purses or dragging their children outside for a good telling-off, and all the time the cash registers were ringing, ringing, ringing. Marvella's had never sold so much, so fast, and, as stocks of favourite toys ran low, tempers began to fray. Brothers and sisters squabbled over their presents, children fell out over a last Pocket Princess or Gotcha Goo-Machine, and desperate parents started swiping toys out of other people's trolleys the moment their backs were turned.

Never had the nation's children been so utterly miserable. But not everybody was miserable. No, some people were not miserable at all. In a sugar-pink house on top of a hill a party was in full swing.

And what a party! There were clowns, puppet shows, a bouncy castle, party-poppers – it was every child's dream! Except there was not a single child in sight. Only a crowd of grinning grown-ups and, at the centre of it all, in a glittering tiara, the party-princess herself – Marvella Brand.

Marvella tinkled on the edge of her glass with her fairy wand. 'Friends!' she chirruped. 'A toast to our success!' The party guests raised their glasses. 'I always knew that children were the most excellent customers,' she smiled, a frosty hardness round the edge of her lips. 'They truly are the most ravenous little monsters, the most grasping little gremlins.' The guests shifted uneasily at these cruel words. 'Yes indeed,' Marvella continued, her voice tart with bitterness, 'every single one of them is nothing but a bottomless pit of greed!' Marvella paused for breath and saw that her guests were looking

TILLS

extremely uncomfortable. It was time to turn back on the charm. She smiled sweetly. 'Which is excellent news for us, of course!' she giggled. The guests chuckled in relief. She was only joking. Wasn't she? 'To children!' Marvella cried, raising a goblet of pink lemonade high in the air.

'To children!' the guests echoed back.

'And to the person who has helped the little rascals reach their full potential – to the brainbox of the century, Dr Calus Gore.'

The audience whooped and cheered, but the brainbox of the century wasn't listening. He was having far too much fun on the bouncy castle.

'Happy Christmas to me! Happy Christmas to me!' he chuckled as he somersaulted through the air. Watching all those glassy-eyed children marching to the shops had been enormous fun. Indeed, Dr Gore hadn't had so much fun since the time he fried a column of ants under a magnifying glass. *So why stop at Britain?* he thought to himself. With this kind of success he could conquer Europe, Asia, America, the world! He felt unstoppable, all-powerful, like an evil Santa Claus.

'He sees you when you're sleeping!' he sang gleefully to himself. 'He knows when you're awake!' He turned a full backflip then belted out the chorus. 'CALUS GORE is coming to town!' he sang. 'CALUS GORE is coming to town! CA-LUS-GORE-IS-COM-ING-TO-TOOOOWN!' And this time no twerpy little school kids were going to stop him.

Deep in the forest, Frankie and his gang sat silently around an old radio listening to reports of the rampages in high streets up and down the country. Rain had started to pour down and large globs of water were splashing through the holes in the roof and on to Frankie's head. Frankie had never felt glummer. He felt like he had failed. That it was all his fault. They hadn't managed to find Wes and Dr Gore had turned children everywhere into zombies. It was a catastrophe. Frankie felt a hand squeeze his knee.

'Patience, little cabbage,' said Alphonsine, looking at him like a concerned sheep-dog. 'We will find a way.' Frankie looked at her and shrugged. He really couldn't see it. What could they do? Wes was their only hope of defeating Dr Gore, but they didn't have the first idea where he was. The whole country had gone Marvella-mad, and all they could do was watch.

'Yes, Frankie!' Alphonsine insisted. 'Zere is *always* a way. Sometimes you cannot see it. Sometimes it is hidden like a mole in a hole. But often, ze answer, it is right there under your schnozzle.'

Suddenly, something seemed to click into place in Frankie's brain.

'What did you just say, Alfie?' he asked.

'Right under your schnozz!' she smiled.

'No, just before that,' Frankie replied.

'Umm . . . I said that ze answer is often hidden, invisible – but it is always there!'

Frankie's eyes lit up.

'You know,' he said with a grin, 'I think you might be right!'

Frankie snatched Wes's postcard off the worktop and ran outside, where the rain was falling most heavily.

'What are you doing, Frankie?' asked Neet, confused. Colette barked with excitement as Frankie held the postcard out under the falling rain. As the raindrops splashed across the card, a transformation took place. Wesley's handwriting started to wash away, but as the ink dripped off the surface another, fainter message began to appear.

'Invisible ink!' smiled Frankie. 'That's why Wes kept going on about the rain. Look!'

The gang held their breath as the letters slowly sharpened before their eyes.

It was an address. Alphonsine gasped in surprise. 'I know that place,' she whispered.

CHAPTER TWENTY-TWO
THE ELVES

'Marvella's Elves: Children's Home,' Frankie read aloud. 'How do you know it, Alfie?'

'I worked at that address many moonshines ago,' Alphonsine replied, stroking her chin. 'I was a carer there, before I became a nanny. But it was just a normal children's home back then. Nothing to do with that horrid Marvella.'

'What's a children's home?' asked Neet.

'It is a place for kiddlers who have no family to look after zem,' Alphonsine explained. 'The children's home looks after zem instead.'

‘That must be how Wes ended up there,’ said Frankie. ‘His parents went missing on safari, didn’t they?’

‘But what is Marvella doing getting mixed up in children’s homes?’ Neet frowned.

Alphonsine raised two suspicious eyebrows. ‘A tip-top question, Neety,’ she said. ‘It is fishier than a crabcake!’

The rain was sloshing down in buckets so the team went back inside to plot their next move.

‘We need to get Wes out of there,’ said Frankie, shaking his head. He dreaded to think what could be happening to his friend. ‘Straight away!’

‘Right!’ said Neet, grabbing her motorcycle helmet. ‘I’m ready! Let’s go!’

Colette howled and pawed at the door.

‘Not so speedy, Neety,’ warned Alphonsine.

'First we must make plans. The children's home is not so easy to break into. The walls are very high and the gate is locked and bolted at night.'

'Maybe we could squeeze through the gates,' said Frankie.

'Not on your nelly,' Alphonsine replied, solemnly shaking her head. 'If you could squeeze in, then the children could squeeze out. No, no, it is shut tight as an oyster.'

The team put their thinking caps on. Neet wondered if Colette could dig a tunnel under the wall. But it would have taken far too long. Eddie thought they might pull the gates off with the motorbike. But they couldn't risk waking anyone inside. They had to get in and out as quickly and quietly as thieves. Frankie wandered round the workshop racking his brains as the others tossed ideas back and forth. The workbenches were littered with sawn-off chunks of wood and rusty old tools. But nothing looked especially helpful. He touched a saw with the tip of his finger and leapt back in alarm – ouch! It was still as sharp as a razor. As he leapt backwards he startled a noisy family of sparrows nesting in an open drawer.

'Shhh, Frankie!' called Neet. 'We're trying to think!'

'Sorry,' Frankie replied, sucking lightly on his bleeding finger. Then, as he watched the sparrows disappearing through the roof, his eyes were drawn to a very odd-looking contraption suspended from the rafters. He stepped towards it to get a closer look. It looked like a cross between a bird and a bicycle. There were wheels and pedals attached to what looked like two large, broken umbrella frames covered with oily feathers. Frankie had seen something like this in a book he read about famous inventors from long ago. His gaze travelled across the ceiling of the workshop. Dozens of bizarre-looking contraptions dangled from the beams like bats in a cave.

'Hey!' Frankie called to his friends, pointing at the strange inventions that hovered over them. 'Look!'

'Oooooooh!' cooed Neet, springing to her feet. She immediately saw what they were. 'Flying-machines!'

'Of course,' said Eddie, shuffling over to take a look. 'These must be the contraptions Mr Whittle was working on before that unfortunate journey to Valkrania.' Alphonsine whipped her spanner from her apron, sprang up on to the workbench and began to inspect.

'But the trouble is,' sighed Eddie, 'Mr Whittle never did manage to make a success of it. These are all failures, I'm afraid.'

'But Alfie can fix them up, can't you, Alfie?'

said Neet hopefully. She couldn't think of anything better than learning to fly.

Alphonsine hummed and hawed and chewed her lip. She was an ace mechanic but this was a challenge.

'It doesn't need to be a super-jet,' said Neet. 'We just need to get over the wall. Please, Alfie – it's our only chance of finding Wes!'

'It is possible,' said Alphonsine cautiously. 'But it will be very dangerous! Very tricksy indeed. We do not want any nasty smash-landings!'

Frankie inspected a particularly flimsy-looking contraption and gulped.

'Oh wow! ' grinned Neet, clapping her hands together in excitement.

Alphonsine fetched a rickety ladder and hauled a slightly sturdier-looking machine down to the floor. Eddie nodded. This one looked promising. But there was work to be done.

Alphonsine dusted her hands together and got down to business. Frankie and Neet passed her a series of tools as she tweaked and wrenched with her spanner, oiled the joints and glued a clutch of feathers back into place.

After an hour of sawing, tightening, sanding and taping, Alphonsine stood back and planted her fists firmly on her hips. It was as ready as it could possibly be, but she looked worried.

'It will fly,' she said. 'Short distances. But it is very perilsome. It will take three small children at most – you two and Wes. No more.' She wrung her hands tightly.

'It'll be fine, Alfie!' chirruped Neet, already clambering into the pilot's seat. 'I can totally see how this thing works, easy-peasy!' But Frankie didn't feel quite so confident. Heights made him queasy, like that time he got stuck on the diving board at the pool. Neet gave him a little nudge.

'Don't worry, Frankie,' she winked. 'You pedal, I'll steer. That way you don't even have to keep your eyes open.' Frankie breathed a sigh of relief. 'Now let's go get Wes!'

'Right!' said Alphonsine. 'Time to put a stop to Dr Gore, once and forever!'

'Yes,' said Frankie, feeling braver, 'once and forever.'

CHAPTER TWENTY-THREE
THE WIRE

It was past midnight by the time they arrived outside the high walls of the children's home. An eerie moon floated above them like a huge white fish and, gleaming in its dim light, was a large steel plaque.

MARVELLA'S ELVES: CHILDREN'S HOME
Generously sponsored by the
Marvella Brand Foundation

Frankie shivered. 'Is it how you remember it, Alfie?' he whispered.

Alphonsine wrinkled her nose and turned down the corners of her mouth, so that she looked like an old stone gargoyle. 'When I was here,' she said, pointing at the top of the brick walls, 'there was none of *that* nonsense.'

Frankie glanced up and saw that the walls were topped with a dense mesh of barbed wire that glinted meanly under the stars. Frankie and Neet gulped. They had to make sure that the flying-machine climbed high enough to make a clear sweep over those walls, or else they would both be ripped to ribbons.

Alphonsine declared that they would need a good, long run-up to get off the ground, so Frankie and Neet dragged the machine up the muddy banks of a neighbouring hillside to give themselves the best chance of making it over the wall without ending up in a deadly tangle of wire. They only had one shot, so it had to be good.

Neet clambered on to the front and took the controls. Alphonsine carefully explained how everything worked while Frankie steadied his feet on the pedals.

'Have courage, little cabbages!' urged Alphonsine, as they got ready to push. Then, before Frankie could change his mind, they were off! Eddie and Alphonsine pushed with all their might, Frankie pressed down hard on the pedals and the machine rushed down the slope like a runaway train. The harder Frankie pedalled the faster the wings flapped – one-two, one-two, one-two! But the machine didn't seem to be rising, only hurtling faster and faster towards the high brick wall. The contraption was shaking so violently Frankie thought his bones would pop out of their sockets.

'Neet!' he shouted. 'Neet! We're not going to make it! We have to bail out!'

But Neet could feel the front of the machine beginning to lift.

'Keep pedalling, Frankie!' she called. 'Pedaaaal!!'

The machine lurched over a clod of grass then, all of a sudden, the shaking stopped and they were lifted up, up, up into the air.

'Woooooooooaah!' Frankie yelled, as the ground disappeared beneath them.

But they weren't safe yet. Alphonsine may have improved Crispin Whittle's invention but flying was no easy feat. The machine did not soar like an eagle, rather it fluttered and flapped like a startled chicken, swerving and lurching in all directions. Neet clung to the controls and pulled the machine up with all the strength she had. But the wall was approaching fast. Frankie couldn't look, he closed his eyes and powered his legs round and round as fast as he was able. Neet gave a shrill cry and at that moment Frankie felt something cold and sharp trace a quick line across his ankle. He gasped in pain but didn't stop pedalling and pedalling until, suddenly, they were bouncing and skidding to a halt.

Frankie opened his eyes. They were on the flat roof of the children's home – all in one piece. Well almost. Frankie felt a warm trickle in his sock. He dabbed his ankle with his fingers. They had skimmed so close to the wire that a sharp barb had left a bleeding slash across his skin. Frankie gulped. If Neet hadn't steered so carefully they would have come to a very sticky end indeed. Luckily, the wound was only shallow so Frankie pulled up his sock and climbed, trembling, out of his seat.

'Nice one, Neety,' he whispered. Neet was shaking with exhaustion. But she was OK. Now it was time to find Wes.

Frankie and Neet spotted a fire escape on top

of the roof and lowered themselves down the steep ladder into the building. Inside, it was as dark as the belly of a whale.

'I can't see a thing!' Neet whispered nervously. 'Where's the light switch?'

'Hang on,' said Frankie. 'We don't want to wake anyone. Have you got the moonglasses?' Neet rummaged blindly in her rucksack and pulled out two pairs. They slipped them over their noses and took a look around. The moonglasses allowed them to see through the darkness like a pair of prowling tomcats. And what they saw made them shudder.

You'd probably expect a children's home to be full of fun things for kids: brightly-coloured paintings, toy chests, playrooms. But there was no such joy at *Marvella's Elves*. Everything about the place was hard and grey. The sombre walls and long, bleak corridors reminded Frankie of a prison, not a home. Even the air seemed leaded with gloom. He saw that the walls were dotted with stern-looking notices: *'DO NOT RUN'*, *'DO NOT TALK'*, *'DO NOT BE LATE'*. He gulped: even Mrs Pinkerton wasn't *that* strict. Neet pointed to a map of the building that was pinned to the wall nearby. Frankie studied the plans. Deep down in the basement, a couple of levels underground, was a series of long thin rooms marked *'DORMITORIES'*. Neet heaved a trembling sigh. 'I think that's where we'll find him.'

As they crept silently down the stairs, Frankie felt as if a cold hand had gripped his heart and was squeezing it tighter and tighter. This place, he thought, had not heard a single laugh, not a single giggle or titter for a very long time. He found it hard to believe that there were actually children living within those walls. In fact, Frankie hardly expected to find anyone at all in those stern, silent surroundings. It was like one of those planets that scientists talk about on the telly – planets that are 'hostile to life'. This whole place felt like it was 'hostile to life' and it made Frankie's skin creep.

'Shhh!' Neet whispered suddenly as they approached the bottom of the stairs. There was a door ahead of them with a small sign outside: '*WARDEN*'. Frankie crept closer and carefully peeked through the window. He saw an immensely round lady in a grey smock wedged into an armchair and snoring like a cement mixer. They were safe – for now. The two friends slipped quickly past in their silent sneakers and stole down the corridor towards the dormitories.

The dormitories were long and cold with rows of bunks stacked with sleeping children. Frankie and Neet crept quickly through them, taking care not to make a sound. But they needn't have worried – nothing could have woken those sleepers. Indeed, Frankie had never seen anyone sleep like those children slept. There was no snoring or tossing and turning. The pale faces that poked above the thin grey blankets were as motionless as waxworks and their limbs were so tired, so heavy, it was as if their bodies had been nailed to the beds.

'Wait,' whispered Neet, stopping dead in her tracks. She pointed to a small, huddled shape on a lower bunk. A tuft of ginger hair sprouted above the blanket. Frankie's heart turned a somersault of joy.

'Wes!' Neet whispered, running to the bedside and shaking the sleeping boy's shoulder. 'We're here, wake up!'

The bundle jolted in surprise and a pale hand scrabbled around on the floor for a pair of glasses. The glasses were pushed on to a freckly nose and a pair of magnified brown eyes blinked anxiously. It was Wes.

As soon as Wes recognised them his face broke into an enormous smile.

'You made it!' he whispered. 'I knew you would!'

The friends hugged silently. Frankie could feel that Wes was very thin around the ribs.

'So you solved my riddle!' Wes whispered.

'We did,' smiled Frankie, noticing the dark circles around his friend's eyes, 'but it wasn't exactly easy to crack! Make it a bit easier next time, will you?'

'Yeah,' smiled Neet, nudging him, 'we don't all have your brains, you know!'

'Sorry,' Wes whispered. 'But the warden checks all our letters to make sure we don't say anything about what goes on here.' Frankie thought he felt the room temperature drop.

'What does go on here?' he asked. The colour drained from Wesley's cheeks.

'It's Dr Gore,' he whispered, 'he's back.'

'We know,' Neet nodded.

'I'll show you,' said Wes, 'then we need to put a stop to it all.'

Neet and Frankie followed Wes through the maze-like corridors of the building. Wes scurried ahead, glancing about him like a nervous squirrel.

'You have to remember,' he whispered, 'that no one cares about the kids here. Most of us don't have parents. No one knows where we are, and no one misses us.' Wes led them across a steel walkway to a separate part of the building. Frankie strained his ears. He could hear the distant whirring and clanking of heavy machinery. It grew louder and louder, like the sound of an approaching train.

'Keep quiet and stay low,' said Wes. 'You mustn't be seen.'

'Isn't everyone in bed?' said Frankie. Wes gave a small, grim smile.

'No,' he replied, shaking his head, 'it never stops.'

They reached a large metal door plastered with scary-looking warning signs. Frankie and Neet got down on their hands and knees as Wes pushed the door open a crack.

What Frankie then saw chilled him to the centre of his bones.

CHAPTER TWENTY-FOUR
THE WHEELS

As soon as the door opened, Frankie's eardrums were pounded by a deafening hammering and screeching. The children squeezed through the gap and crawled out on to a narrow steel ledge with an iron-mesh floor that cut into their knees and the palms of their hands. Frankie took off his moonglasses and peered down through the railings. They were high up over an enormous hangar-like space that was large enough for an aeroplane to park in. It was packed to the rafters with a giant tangle of machinery. Long conveyor belts whizzed up, down and around, transporting hundreds of multicoloured packages. Giant brass pipes and drums puffed and belched out clouds of steam. Cranes as tall as giraffes hoisted heavy boxes into large steel containers. And amongst all this unstoppable machine-power, hundreds of small, pink fingers were working away, sealing packaging, packing boxes and pulling levers.

'It's a factory!' whispered Neet. 'A toy factory!'

'Right,' said Wes. 'This is where Marvella's toys are made.'

Marvella's toy factory was nothing like the magical workshops you see on the front of Christmas cards. There was no jolly Santa and no merry little helpers. Instead, Marvella's factory was staffed by row upon row of exhausted-looking children, many younger than Frankie himself. The children's hands and arms moved so precisely and mechanically you could almost believe that they were part of the machines. In fact, they seemed as lifeless as the animatronic elves Frankie had seen in the grotto. As the machines whirred and throbbed, the children moved in synch, staring straight ahead of them with eyes like blown lightbulbs. Frankie shrank back in alarm. The lanes between the children's workbenches were patrolled by wardens with swivelling eyes, each of whom carried a mean-looking rod that would snap down on tired little fingers the moment they paused for rest.

'Good grief,' Frankie whispered, lost for words.

Frankie's gaze travelled to the edge of the factory. All along the walls were what looked like enormous spinning hamster wheels. At first Frankie couldn't work out what he was seeing. Or maybe he just couldn't believe it. Each wheel was powered by a child running round and round as fast as they could go, sweat pouring down their foreheads.

'What on earth are those?' whispered Frankie.

'Those are the Wheels,' Wes replied. 'They power the machinery. Dr Gore invented them.'

'No kidding,' said Neet, grimly remembering Dr Gore's days as a classroom pet. 'I guess it is some kind of revenge.'

Frankie shook his head in dismay. The whole scene reminded him of some books he had read about the lives of children many, many years ago, long before Alphonsine was born. Back in those days children used to be sent down mines and would spend all day in the dark, on their hands and knees, scratching out lumps of coal. Or they would be made to work in factories like this one, stitching, stamping or weaving until the joints in their fingers ached and their brains turned to slop. Frankie didn't think that such a thing could be allowed to happen any more. But Dr Gore was capable of anything.

Neet saw that one production line was packaging Mechanimal schoolbags like the one she had picked out for Frankie.

'Look!' she whispered. 'Mechanimal schoolbags! That's where we found your note, Wes.' Wes nodded.

'I must have sent hundreds of them,' he said. 'We've all been trying to get messages to the outside, but nobody responded until now. I guess everyone was too excited by their new toys to notice. It's so lucky you recognised my writing, Neet, because . . . because if you hadn't . . .' Wesley's voice tailed off and his eyes darkened momentarily as if a shadow had passed behind them,

'OK, Wes,' said Frankie. 'We need to get you out of here.' Wes looked worried.

'I can't go by myself,' he whispered anxiously. 'What about everybody else? We can't leave them here!'

'We'll come back for them, Wes, don't you worry,' said Neet, putting her arm around his thin shoulders. 'But we can only take one person with us tonight. There's not enough room for more.'

Frankie nodded in agreement. 'And you're the only one who can stop Dr Gore.'

As they clambered back on to the roof, Frankie and Neet told Wes everything. They told him about the Mechanimals and Crispin Whittle's workshop and *Project Wishlist*. By the time they had finished, Wes looked as white as a goose.

'So what you're saying is . . .' he gulped, 'Dr Gore has already won. He's turned everyone into zombies.'

'It's not over yet,' Frankie replied. 'We can find

a way to reverse the process. I'm sure we can. But we need your help, Wes. You're the only one who knows about computers and digital stuff.' Wes couldn't suppress a proud smile. Yes indeed, he knew a lot about computers and digital stuff. He listened carefully as Frankie told him about the mind-sweepers and the computer laboratory at Marvella's headquarters where they turned children's brains into billboards.

'OK,' said Wes, 'I think we can do it.'

Inky clouds had blotted out the moon and stars. The friends climbed on to the flying-machine and prepared themselves for take-off. Wes hopped into the remaining saddle and put his feet in the stirrups. But even with Wes's extra pedal-power, with no one to push them they would have to work extra hard to lift themselves up off the edge of the roof and over the wire-topped walls. Frankie touched his ankle. The blood had dried, but he didn't fancy taking any risks. On the count of three Frankie pumped his legs round and round as fast as he could while Neet held a steady course. As they sped towards the edge of the roof the wings began to move up and down and up and down. Then, as if the machine were as light as a feather, it lifted gracefully off the ground.

'We're getting better at this!' cried Neet.

But at that moment, Frankie suddenly felt his feet jam and the machine jerk. Somebody had grabbed on to the back. Frankie glanced down and saw a pair of round blue eyes blinking up at him in terror. It was Timmy.

CHAPTER TWENTY-FIVE
THE CRASH

'Let go, Timmy!' Frankie yelled as the flying-machine lurched and dived like a dozy duck. 'We'll come back for you later! For all of you!' But it was too late. They were already way up high in the air. If Timmy let go now he'd end up splattered like a raspberry ripple on the ground below. Timmy's fingers clutched and clawed at the back of the saddle.

'Oooooeeeeeee!' he yelled, as he was flung left and right and shaken about like an old duster. Neet struggled to control the machine while

Frankie pedalled so hard he thought his legs might never stop. As the machine ducked and plunged, Wes turned himself around and grabbed on to Timmy's wrists.

'Quick!' Wes called in panic. 'He's slipping!' Wes was right. Timmy's hands were so damp with sweat they were fast losing their grip.

'Heeeeeeeelp!' Timmy squealed, his eyes widening in fear. 'Heeeeeeelp meeeeeeee!'

Frankie squeezed his eyes tight as Timmy's dangling legs just missed the barbed wire mesh. They were over, but the danger had not yet passed. Frankie could feel the gear-box straining like a carthorse. Then suddenly, there was an ear-splitting crack just above his head. He looked up to see one of the fragile wings tear off and go spinning down to the ground, where it broke into a dozen mangled pieces. Neet tried desperately to wrestle back control but the machine was spinning and screeching like a cat in a dryer. Frankie could no longer tell which way was up and which way was down. As they hurtled through the cold night air, the whole world seemed to blur into speeding, multicoloured stripes. Neet shouted something at the top of her voice, then Frankie heard a terrific shattering sound as if somebody had broken a dinner plate on his head.

After that . . .

. . . nothing . . .

. . . blackout . . .

. . . silence.

The next feeling Frankie was aware of was a cold, mossy smell in his nostrils. He opened one bleary eye and swivelled it slowly around. It was still night time. His face was pressed up against some wet bark and his limbs were dangling in space.

'Euuuurgh!' he grumbled, rubbing his sore head. 'Where am I?'

He glanced downwards and his stomach clenched like a fist. He was high above the ground, caught in the branches of a sycamore tree. From where he was lying, he could just about see the remains of the flying-machine scattered far below. Frankie took a deep breath and focussed his eyes on the branch in front of him. As his head began to steady, he remembered the terrifying descent. 'Where are the others?' he gasped.

He sat up straight and looked up through the branches, searching for his friends. He soon spotted Neet and Wes, who were perching on a higher branch, rubbing their heads and inspecting their bruises.

'You OK?' Frankie shouted up to them.

'Just about,' Neet replied. 'Where's Timmy?'

Frankie looked around, but couldn't see a trace

of him. Then, just as he was suspecting the worst, he heard a soft snivelling coming from behind a cluster of leaves. Frankie pushed the branches aside. There was Timmy, dangling upside-down, suspended by a single shoelace that had become caught in the branches.

'Stay still, Timmy,' said Frankie, worried that the shoelace might snap. But Timmy was far too upset to listen.

'I'm sorry . . . I'm sorry, Frankie . . .' he burbled. 'I'm sorry everyone.'

'You almost got us killed!' Neet shouted down crossly. Large blue tears spilled from Timmy's eyes. But these ones weren't phoney.

'I know,' he said. 'I'm sorry. I had to get out of there. I'm sorry for everything.'

'It's all right, Timmy,' said Frankie, who could see the shoelace thinning fast. 'Try to keep still.'

Frankie shuffled along the branch to get

closer. But Timmy hadn't finished. The apologies kept coming in big salty waves.

'I'm sorry for being so mean to you,' he burbled, 'for leaving you out and everything. It's just that . . . I was new and . . . if I didn't have so many toys . . . nobody would want to play with me.' Timmy let out a short sob. 'They only play with me because I have all the best toys.'

Frankie couldn't believe his ears. He had never seen Timmy in such a state. Timmy who was always so popular, so sure of himself. Little Timmy Snodgrass, prince of the playground.

The shoelace was unravelling fast and looked set to snap.

'Keep still, Timmy!' Frankie yelled. But it was too late.

'They call me Timmy Snotty-paaaaaaants!' Timmy bawled, as he plummeted towards the ground.

'Timmy!' Frankie shouted after him in horror. He squeezed his eyes shut and held his breath. As he waited to hear the terrible thud, he felt as if his heart had stopped beating. *Poor Timmy!* he thought. *Poor, poor Timmy Snottypants.* Frankie had been so upset by Timmy's teasing, it had never occurred to him that Timmy might also be afraid – afraid of not being popular enough, of not really being liked, of not having any real friends. And now he was going to end up, splattered like an egg, on the ground below.

But the thud didn't come. Frankie gulped and peered down through the branches, terrified of what he might see. And he was right to be terrified. In the dim glare of the moonlight, he saw two furious grey eyes looking right back at him.

'Ach!' shouted a cross French accent. 'What did I tell you? That machine was never meant for four whole kiddlers!' Alphonsine was standing at the foot of the tree holding a trembling Timmy in her arms.

Frankie felt his whole body flood with relief. He had never been so happy to see little Timmy Snodgrass. He thought he might actually dissolve with joy. Frankie forgot his fear of heights and, laughing loudly, he began to swing himself back down to the ground.

'It is no giggling matter, Frankie!' puffed Alphonsine. 'You is lucky! Very lucky you is not dead as a doughnut!'

'Sorry, Alfie,' said Frankie, as his feet touched the earth. Alphonsine shook her head in annoyance then placed Timmy gently on the grass.

As Alphonsine and Eddie helped the others out of the tree, Frankie sat down next to Timmy, who was trembling like a bag of jelly.

'It's all right, Timmy,' said Frankie. 'You're safe now.' Timmy looked at Frankie with large wet eyes.

'I'm sorry . . .' he sniffled, 'really sorry. Do you forgive me?'

'Sure I do,' said Frankie, without hesitation. He could see that this time Timmy meant every word he said. Neet and Wes wandered over to where the two of them were sitting. 'We're your friends. Aren't we, guys?'

'Of course,' smiled Neet, 'and believe me – it's not because of your toys!'

'Really?' Timmy sniffled.

'Absolutely,' said Neet. 'I never want to see another toy again in my life!'

'Me neither,' said Timmy. 'And you know what? As soon as I get home, my letter to Santa is going straight in the bin – all twenty pages of it!'

The children giggled with relief and exhaustion. But there was no time to rest.

'We've got a lot of work to do,' said Frankie, checking his watch. 'We need to get to the computer lab at Marvella's before dawn and undo all the damage Gore has done. It's time to put a stop to all this.' He looked at Timmy. 'Are you coming with us?' Timmy smiled and wiped away his tears.

'Oh yes,' he said. 'Count me in!'

CHAPTER TWENTY-SIX
THE CLEAN-UP

Frankie fidgeted nervously. They were in the computer lab at Marvella's headquarters, surrounded by dozens of blinking monitors. Wes had set to work on the computer systems, Alphonsine, Eddie and Colette were waiting below on the getaway bike and Timmy kept lookout at the door. Frankie parted the office blinds with his fingers. The morning star was glowing ever more brightly on the horizon. He let the blinds snap shut and let out a shaky sigh. Wes had been tapping away at the computers for a couple of hours now, but Frankie had no idea if he was making any progress.

'How's it going, Wes?' he asked, cracking his knuckles anxiously. Wes was glued to the monitors, his fingers flying over the keyboards like tap-dancing spiders.

'Getting there . . .' he said, '. . . slowly. If I can hack into Dr Gore's account then I should be able to delete all the Marvella logos from the hard drive.' Frankie scratched his head. He wasn't sure he understood.

'You mean you can get everyone's memories back to the way they were?'

'That's right,' said Wes, his fingers still tapping away. 'Then we can send those memories back to the Mechanimals and the whole process will be reversed.'

'Can we delete all the Marvella logos from children's memories tonight?' asked Neet.

'Everyone is still asleep,' Wes nodded. 'So we should be able to do it before sunrise.'

'Genius,' smiled Neet. Wes blushed with pride. Then his face lit up like a beacon.

'That's it!' he exclaimed. 'I'm in!'

Dr Gore's log-in page flashed on to the screen. It displayed a photograph of the scientist on holiday wearing a rubber ring in the shape of a duck. Frankie spluttered with laughter, but there was no time for giggles. Wes was working so fast that Frankie couldn't keep track of all the clicking and tapping. Then, after ten minutes or so, he touched down triumphantly on the keyboard.

'It's working,' he said, pointing at the monitors. Frankie looked up at the screens that panelled the walls of the room. Dozens of children's memories flashed past at high speed as if they were on fast-forward. As they sped by, Frankie saw birthday parties, visits to grandparents, sports days and school playtimes all crudely splattered with Marvella Brand logos and Marvella Brand toys. But Wes's reprogramming seemed to be working. As soon as the memories appeared, the logos were rapidly erased. Frankie breathed a long sigh of relief.

'These cleaned-up memories are being sent straight back to the Mechanimals,' said Wes, still tapping at the keyboard. 'Within the next half hour, the Mechanimals will restore everyone's memories and everything should be back to normal.' Frankie punched the air with joy.

'You did it, Wes!' Frankie laughed. 'You did it! It's over! Neet, it's over!' But Neet didn't look so sure.

'What's up?' said Frankie, deflated. 'It's over . . . isn't it?' Neet shrugged her shoulders.

'For now,' she said glumly, 'but Dr Gore is still out there. What's going to stop him doing this all over again, or worse?' Neet was right. It was just a matter of time before Gore hatched another evil plot in that swollen brain of his.

'I agree. But what can we do?' said Wes shaking his head in despair. 'We'd need a whole army to stop Dr Gore.'

Suddenly, Frankie had an idea. Maybe the best idea he had ever had.

Neet's grin spread wider and wider as Frankie explained his plan. 'Brilliant,' she smiled. 'I think that's the best idea you've ever had!'

'Do you think you can do that, Wes?' asked Frankie.

'Easy-peasy,' nodded Wes, flicking back to the photograph of Dr Gore on holiday. 'All I need is this photo here, and I can do that straight away . . .'

'Fantastic!' smiled Neet, clapping her hands together. 'Gore won't know what hit him!'

But Wes's fingers had barely touched the

keyboard when a red-faced Timmy burst into the room.

'Guards!' he burbled, waving his arms in the air. 'We need to leave! Quickly!'

'Just one second . . .' Wes replied, tapping away furiously.

'No, really!' squeaked Timmy, turning pale. 'We have to go! Right now!' But Wes wouldn't be torn away from the keyboard. He was almost there . . . almost there . . .

'And . . . it's . . . DONE!' he cried. 'OK. Let's get out of here!'

But it was too late.

The doorway darkened. There was no way out. Marvella's henchmen, Donner and Blitzen, stormed in and seized a child in each of their massive fists. Frankie kicked and wriggled in panic as the guards hauled them down to an underground car park and tossed them into the back of a waiting van. Frankie saw that there was somebody in the driver's seat.

'Help! Help us!' he yelled, rattling the bars that separated him from the driver. But the driver was doing no such thing. He turned his head to inspect his captives with his strange yellow eyes. His moustache twitched with amusement. It was Dr Calus Gore.

The children howled and hammered on the doors with their fists as the van screeched out of the car park and sped off down the motorway.

'Where are you taking us!' yelled Neet.

'Ah ha!' grinned Dr Gore, as if he were planning a lovely surprise. 'That is for me to know and for you to find out. Don't be so impatient, Miss Banerjee.'

Frankie stared through the cloudy windows at the back of the van, wondering if he could smash through them. But it was useless. Even if he could, they would only end up splat in the middle of the motorway. Frankie felt a wave of despair rising in his throat.

But then he heard a sound he knew only too well. At that moment it was the most wonderful sound in the world – the ferocious growl of a motorbike engine. Frankie pressed his nose to the glass. A few hundred yards behind them, a large black bike roared into view. Alphonsine, Eddie and Colette were on their tail and catching up fast. The children all glued themselves to the window, yelling and waving frantically. Yes! Alphonsine had seen them and gave them a sly wink from behind her goggles. But Gore had seen her too. He put his foot on the gas and swerved left and right through the traffic, chuckling like a demented chipmunk.

'Just you wait!' Neet yelled, as she was hurled from one side of the van to another. 'Alphonsine won't listen to any of your nonsense!'

'Oh I'm not worried about that old handbag,'

sneered Dr Gore, his mouth turning sourly at the corners like the skin of a dried lemon.

'What do you mean?' said Frankie, feeling a strange sense of dread spreading through his limbs.

'I thought she might be sticking her old proboscis in,' the scientist sighed. 'So I had Rudolph do a little work on that banger of hers. Simple little trick – if her motorbike goes over seventy miles per hour, its tyres will burst.' He made a small exploding gesture with his fingers. 'POP!'

The friends all gasped in horror.

'You're crazy!' shouted Neet, flinging herself at the bars with rage. 'Completely bonkers!'

Dr Gore chuckled. 'Perhaps you're right, Miss Banerjee.' Then his grin turned into a steely snarl as he pushed his foot down on the pedal.

Frankie started to panic. He could see the trembling needle of the speedometer creeping slowly upwards as they approached a high bridge over a wide, cold river. Sixty-six . . . Sixty-seven . . . Sixty-eight . . .

Frankie flew to the back of the van and started signalling wildly for Alphonsine to slow down. Alphonsine and Eddie looked back at him with puzzled expressions. Only Colette seemed to understand. The white pom-pom on the end of her tail stopped wagging. She looked up at Alphonsine with two wet eyes and howled for all she was worth. But it was too late.

As they struck out across the bridge, Frankie heard a chilling bang. Then everything seemed to move in slow motion. Alphonsine's bike spun out of control and, as Frankie looked helplessly on, it lurched over the edge of the bridge and disappeared from view.

Frankie felt as if he had been plunged underwater. His vision went blurry, his ears seemed blocked off and he couldn't breathe.

Chapter Twenty-Seven
The Polar Princess

'They'll be OK . . .' Neet stammered, not knowing what else to say. 'You know Alphonsine. They'll have swum to safety. I'm sure . . .' Frankie nodded silently and squeezed her hand. He couldn't bear to think about it.

The van stopped sharply, throwing the children to the floor. The two henchmen bundled them out of the back and dumped them on the ground like a pile of bin bags. Frankie sniffed. His nostrils filled with sharp, salty air. Sea air. Looking up, he saw the sides of ships, glaring

MB
MB
MB

white in the morning sun. They were at the docks. Large liners were ploughing in and out of the deep, watery bays while cranes swerved slowly overhead, transporting cargo to the waiting vessels. Frankie sat up and saw that they were surrounded by stacks of steel containers, each of which was stamped with the huge, grinning face of Teddy Manywishes. Frankie shook his head in dismay. The Marvella corporation was preparing to send its mind-mashing toys all around the world. Frankie looked at the sides of ships – India, China, Australia, the USA. Nowhere was safe.

'What are we doing here?' demanded Neet crossly, jumping to her feet and dusting herself off.

'Temper, temper, Miss Banerjee!' Gore smirked. 'I'm sending you all on a little cruise.' Donner and Blitzen sniggered like a pair of mutts.

'But I don't want to go on a cruise!' Timmy

panicked. 'I want to go home! I want to go home!'

Dr Gore rolled his yellow eyes. 'Don't be such moaning minnies,' he snapped. 'You'll have a splendid time. But do watch out for the polar bears, they are a little grouchy at this time of year.'

'P-p-polar bears?' Wesley stuttered. 'You mean, you're sending us to the Arctic?'

'Bravo, Master Jones!' smirked Gore. 'You always were the clever one. Yes indeed, I am sending you to the Arctic. Seeing as you are all incapable of staying out of my way, I shall have to dispose of you along with the other toxic waste.' Dr Gore gestured towards a nearby ship that was loading up with dirty-looking containers full of the filth and rubbish from Marvella's factories.

'But . . . but we'll freeze to death!' Wesley stammered.

'Or we'll be eaten by killer whales!' Neet howled.

'Well, children,' smiled the crazy old scientist as if he were giving them a sermon, 'that will teach you a valuable lesson, won't it? Good children get presents, naughty children get eaten by whales. Such is life.'

The ship's horn gave a long, loud blast. Frankie looked wildly about him for an exit route, but they were blocked in by containers and closely guarded by Donner and Blitzen. *If only Alfie and Eddie were here,* he thought to himself. *They'd know what to do.* Frankie strained his ears, hoping against hope that he would hear the sound of a distant motorbike. But all he heard was the croaking of seagulls and the creak of cranes. Frankie's heart felt as heavy as a stone . . . until . . .

Wait . . .

Listen . . .

Frankie wondered if it was his desperate imagination. But no. He heard something in the distance. It wasn't a motorbike, but he could definitely hear something. Something coming steadily closer. Something unstoppable. Frankie held his breath and glanced across at Wes. Wes was smiling faintly. It looked like their plan was beginning to work.

'Throw them in with the cargo,' snapped Dr Gore.

Donner and Blitzen hoisted all four children off the ground and started to march them towards the gaping black mouth of the cargo hold. The friends shouted and squirmed.

'I don't want to go to the Arctic!' Timmy bawled hysterically. 'I left my mittens at home! I'll catch a cold! Heeeeeeeeelp!'

Then, suddenly, the guards stopped in their

tracks. They turned and looked about them, sniffing the air like a pair of nervous bison.

'Stop dawdling!' snapped Dr Gore. 'Throw them in the cargo hold, chop-chop.' But then Dr Gore heard what they were hearing. His tufty ears pricked up in alarm. They could all hear it. Nearer and nearer, closer and closer – the march of thousands of mechanical feet.

Donner and Blitzen didn't hang about. They dropped the children like hot potatoes, raced to the van and roared away in a billow of dust, leaving Dr Gore to fend for himself. Gore's eyes flashed around him like torch-beams.

'What's going on?' he shrilled. 'What have you done this time, Blewitt?' The sound of footsteps grew louder and louder and the air was filled with a distinctive series of pips and bleeps. Then they arrived. From every direction, from every corner, dozens and dozens of Mechanimals.

Sparky the Squirrels, Gigawatt the Gila Monsters, Gadget the Rabbits – and they were all homing in on Dr Gore.

'What the devil?' Dr Gore spluttered in alarm.

'They've been reprogrammed . . .' Frankie shouted over the clamour, '. . . to recognise *you*. They think you're their owner now.'

'That's right,' yelled Neet. 'You're their new best friend and they'll follow you to the ends of the earth. Whether you like it or not!'

Suddenly the steel containers started to rattle and shake. Dozens of new Mechanimals were tearing themselves out of their packaging and crawling robotically towards their target.

'Get them away from me!' Gore yelled. The Mechanimals' mind-sweepers were switched on and they were aiming directly at Dr Gore's enormous forehead.

'Keep them away from my brain!' The scientist

tried to make a dash for it but every way was blocked. He was completely surrounded by the advancing toys.

Dr Gore was panicking like a snake in a sack.

'Turn them off!' he shouted. 'Take their batteries out!'

But Frankie and his friends stayed right where they were. The Mechanimals wobbled robotically forward, chanting in their high, tinny voices, *'Caaaaluuus! Caaaaaaluuus! Be my frieeeeeend!'*

'Waaaagh!' yelled the scientist, backing himself into a corner. Seeing that his threats weren't working, he tried another strategy. 'Children, children!' he pleaded. 'You're making a big mistake here. You're missing a huge opportunity. We could work together! Think of all the extra pocket money you could make! And the freebies! You'll have freebies coming out of your ears! Just turn off those blasted chunks of plastic!'

'No way!' Frankie shouted back. 'You've done enough harm as it is. It's about time somebody gave *your* mind a makeover!'

Dr Gore saw that the doors to one of the waste containers stood ajar. Quick as a bobcat, he hurled himself inside and slammed the doors shut behind him. Frankie saw his chance. No sooner had the doors closed than he lunged towards the large steel bolt and shoved it across.

'Bleeeeewittt!' shrieked the scientist, immediately realising that he was locked in. 'Banerjeeeeee!'

'Look out!' Neet shouted. Frankie heard a loud whirring of gears and clanking of chains. A crane dangled its giant mechanical claw overhead. Frankie dived out of the way as it grasped hold of the steel box containing Dr Gore, winched it high up in the air and swung it out over the water towards the waiting ship.

‘Woooooooh!’ Dr Gore yelled from inside the container. ‘Let me out! Let me out! I’ll be nice! I promise! I’ll be good! Oooooh, it’s dark in here!’

. . . But only the seagulls could hear him.

As the ship raised its anchor, Frankie read the letters painted along its broad white side: *The Polar Princess*. He smiled drily. Santa would be getting an unexpected visitor this year. The ship pulled slowly out of the harbour and the Mechanimals, still pursuing their target, started marching off the end of the dock. Frankie watched as dozens and dozens of them splashed into the sea where they buzzed and crackled for a moment before sinking like brightly-coloured pebbles. As the ship steamed towards the horizon, Timmy started to jump for joy. ‘We did it! ’ he cheered. ‘We did it! Wowee! Ha ha! It was soooo cool what you did with those Mechanimals, Wes!’

Wes turned pink with pride. 'Oh, it was a piece of cake really,' he said. 'I can do much cleverer things with computers.'

'Really?' said Timmy, impressed. 'Could you teach me?'

'Sure!' grinned Wes. 'What do you want to know?'

While the new friends chatted together, Frankie and Neet sat on the edge of the dock, watching the Mechanimals topple into the water below.

'We did a good job, Frankie,' said Neet, squeezing his shoulder. But Frankie didn't reply. He just watched, pale and silent, as a shiny blue Gadget the Rabbit sank beneath the surface of the water and disappeared from sight. Neet knew there was only one thing on his mind: what had happened to Alphonsine, Eddie and Colette?

CHAPTER TWENTY-EIGHT
THE TYRE

Later that morning, when the children of Britain rubbed the sleep from their eyes, they felt as if they had just awoken from a very long, very eerie dream. They couldn't remember exactly what the dream had been about, but they all had the same, strange feeling that they had not quite been themselves. Some felt as if they had been turned into giant puppets whose strings had been pulled by an invisible hand, while others imagined that they had been transformed into remote-controlled cars or robots. Either way, they were all very glad

MB
10

that it was over. They sat up, looked at their feet, legs and arms and gave themselves a little pinch. Their dads were getting breakfast ready downstairs; their brothers were yelling in the next room. Yes, everything was back to normal.

Except for one thing. Their bedrooms were chock-a-block full of toys. The children rubbed their eyes and looked around in amazement as they struggled to remember how they had all got there. Toy boxes were spilling over, wardrobes were stuffed full to bursting and there were bags and bags of unopened packages littered around their bedrooms. Some of the children noticed that their Mechanimal was missing, but most were simply astounded at the mountains of stuff that was piled all around them. Most of it wasn't even stuff they actually wanted. Little Alice Hinton was baffled by her twenty fluffy unicorns, while Felix Saunders wondered what he was doing with a huge toy battleship. Over the road, Beate Lübecker was mystified by her bumper-bucket of goo, while her classmate, Isabel Stone, was not at all pleased to find a dozen new teddies in her bed while her beloved old rabbit was in the dustbin outside.

What's more, when the children looked at these piles of shopping bags, they began to feel sick, as if they had eaten a whole truckload of marshmallows. They didn't know why, but they could no longer stand the sight of the Marvella logo and even the slightest mention of the toyshop made them feel quite dizzy. Indeed, whenever they saw the grinning face of Teddy Manywishes leering at them from a billboard or the side of a bus, they felt an awful lurch in their stomachs as if they were about to throw up. Parents up and down the country scratched their heads in astonishment. They couldn't work out why their children who, just days ago, had begged and grovelled for the very latest gizmo or gadget, were now turning green at the sight of them. The staff at Marvella's toyshops couldn't believe it either. Only the day before, the cash registers had been ringing non-stop. But that morning there were no crowds pushing against the doors at opening-time, no mobs of squabbling parents and no money going into the tills. Except for the odd whirr of a mechanical toy and the occasional bleep of a video game, the enormous shops were completely silent.

'What happened?' a worried shop assistant asked her friend.

'I don't know,' the friend replied, 'but I don't want to be here when the boss finds out.'

Meanwhile, Frankie and his friends had retraced their steps to the bridge from which Alphonsine's bike had plummeted. Frankie peered anxiously down towards the water as cars and lorries sped close behind him. The bridge was higher than Frankie had imagined. It was at least five times as high as the highest diving board at the swimming pool and the water below looked as solid as steel. Frankie's eyes scanned the surface for any sign of Alfie, Eddie or Colette. Then he saw something that made him freeze inside.

Floating a little way downstream, was the tyre of a motorbike. Neet gasped. 'Oh no, Frankie,' she said, clutching her friend's arm. The motorbike was in pieces. It had broken up as it hit the water and bits of fender, exhaust and engine were scattered across a wide area, glinting cruelly in the cold winter sunshine. Nobody could have survived that fall.

Frankie felt the tears streaming uncontrollably down his cheeks. He ran to the end of the bridge, down the steps and towards the water's edge, hoping with all his heart that he would find something, anything, that would reunite him with his old friends. Neet, Wes and Timmy followed him down and helped him search the river banks. A few bits of bike had washed up on the shore but apart from that there was nothing. Eventually, Frankie slumped down on the shore and sobbed. His friends gathered quietly around him. They didn't know what to say. Timmy saw that Frankie was shivering. He took off his jumper and wrapped it around Frankie's shoulders like a shawl.

Suddenly, Frankie's sobbing spluttered to a halt. He looked up.

'Do you remember what Alphonsine was wearing?' he asked Neet, his eyes wide with hope.

Neet paused to think.

'Not really, Frankie,' she said gently, 'why do you ask?'

Then, all of a sudden, she realised what

Frankie was thinking. They both sprang to their feet. They had been searching for Alphonsine down on the ground, when they should have been looking up in the trees. Frankie's eyes roved over the treetops. There was nothing there. He charged into the nearby woodland.

'Alfiiiiiiiiiiiiie! Eddiiiiiiiiiiiie!' he hollered up into the branches. But only his echo replied. His heart was beginning to sink back down into his socks, when he heard a faint barking.

Frankie ran through the trees with Neet alongside him. He sprang over roots and charged through brambles, not even feeling the scratches on his legs.

A voice rang through the woodlands. 'Yoooohooooo! Little cabbages!'

Frankie looked up and saw Alphonsine, Eddie and Colette high up in a large chestnut tree, suspended by Alphonsine's trusty para-shawl.

'Ooh-la-la!' smiled Alphonsine, who was holding Colette in her arms while Eddie clung on to her ankle. 'At last! We've been dangling here for ages, have we not, Eddie?'

'No, no,' Eddie wheezed politely. 'No trouble at all.' Frankie felt so happy. Happier than he had ever been. Happier than all the Christmas mornings in the world.

Chapter Twenty-Nine
The Scoop

Alfie and Eddie chortled with glee as Frankie and his friends told them how the dastardly Dr Gore had ended up on a slow boat to the Arctic Circle.

'Well done, little cabbages!' grinned Alphonsine, thumping the kitchen table with her fist. 'I knew you could do it! You are all such smartycloggs!'

'Smartypants,' Timmy corrected her.

'Yes, yes,' muttered Alphonsine. 'Smartycloggs, Cleverpants, same thing! Who wants pancakes?'

Everybody wanted pancakes. The friends all

chattered happily as they settled down to fill their growling bellies. Well, almost all of them. Frankie noticed that Wes was strangely quiet.

'Are you all right, Wes?' Frankie asked.

Wes shook his head and pushed his plate away. 'We have to go back for the Elves, Frankie,' he said. 'We can't leave them there a moment longer.'

'Of course,' Frankie nodded, putting down his knife and fork. 'You're right. We'll go back straight away.'

But Wes still looked flustered. 'Only I don't see how we're going to get them out,' he said. 'The flying-machine is in splinters and they'll have tightened up security since our escape.'

Frankie chewed slowly on a blueberry – Wes had a point. But Neet didn't seem worried at all.

'We don't need a flying-machine,' she said. 'Look.' She rolled up her sleeve to reveal the watcher strapped around her wrist.

'What's that?' asked Wes.

'It's a secret camera,' said Neet, winking at Alphonsine. 'For spying. While we were in the factory I took a whole bunch of photos.' She opened the back of the device and took out the film. 'All we need to do now is get this to the newspapers. As soon as people realise what's going on in that place, it'll be shut down for good!'

'Clever, clever Neety!' smiled Alphonsine, tapping Neet on the forehead with her bony old finger. 'You have the makings of a master-spy, no doubts about it!'

That afternoon, Frankie and his friends got on the phone to newspapers, TV channels and radio stations and, within half an hour, a thick buzz of journalists and photographers was swarming excitedly up the driveway.

'What did I tell you?' grinned Neet.

The friends opened the front door to a dazzle of flash-bulbs and, as Alphonsine chased photographers out of her flowerbeds with wide swipes of her broom, the children told the crowd exactly what had happened. They told them how Dr Gore and Marvella Brand had plotted to invade the brains of the world's children and turn them into unthinking, unstoppable toy-monsters. They told them about the Mechanimals and the mind-sweepers and the morse code. And of course they told them about the poor Elves, working their fingers to the bone and running round and round on enormous hamster wheels till they collapsed with exhaustion. The journalists were listening so intently Frankie thought he could see their ears sizzling.

'And here's the proof!' cried Neet triumphantly, holding the roll of film in the air.

A keen-eyed journalist snatched it out of her

hands like a hungry dog and scampered off to get the photos developed, 'We've got a scoop!' he yelped excitedly down the phone to his editor, 'the scoop of the century!'

Just as Neet predicted, the story quickly ballooned into a national outcry. By six o'clock that evening, *Marvella's Elves* had been closed and dazed-looking children wrapped in blankets were being led out into the fresh air. Frankie and his friends were glued to the TV screen as the story unfolded before their eyes.

'There's Martha!' said Wes, tapping the screen with his finger. 'And there's Eric!' Wes's friends were so pale they were almost transparent.

'What's going to happen to them now?' asked Frankie.

'The reporter said they'd be looked after,' Wes replied. 'She said they'd be sent to proper homes.'

'That's great news, Wes!' smiled Frankie, putting his arm around his friend. 'And it's all thanks to you! If you hadn't got that message out . . .' But Wes was only half listening. His eyes were fixed to the screen and he was fiddling nervously with the buttons of his cardigan. Suddenly Frankie realised what was on his mind. How could he have forgotten?

'You can come and live with us, Wes,' said Frankie. 'Isn't that right, Alphonsine?'

Wes looked at his friend with wide eyes. 'Really?' he stammered. 'Are you sure?'

'But of course!' cried Alphonsine. 'We is needing a brainbox like you to teach us all about the interweb, isn't we, Eddie?'

'Absolutely,' said Eddie. 'This old dog is planning to learn a few new tricks!'

'Well,' blushed Wes, smiling, 'I can definitely help you there.'

'Hey, look!' Neet exclaimed, pointing at the TV. The screen showed long queues of people lining up outside Marvella Brand's Happyland. Frankie's heart sank.

'I don't believe it,' he gasped. 'I can't believe people still want to shop there.'

'No, Frankie,' said Neet. 'They're waiting to take stuff back, look!'

Neet was right. What was good news for the journalists was very, very bad news for the Marvella Brand corporation. Not only were children not buying any more Marvella toys, they were marching them straight to the shops and demanding their money back. For the second time in the space of a week, Marvella shop assistants were run off their feet, but rather than putting money in the till, they were handing it back to thousands of unhappy customers. Indeed, Marvella Brand's Happyland was losing business faster than you could flush fifty-pound notes down the toilet. The TV showed dozens of charts with plunging red lines while clench-jawed people in suits spat with fury. Frankie thought he recognised the woman with the pointy shoes. She was talking about 'shares', and 'investments', and saying a lot of words that did not make much sense to Frankie. But he understood one thing loud and clear. Marvella Brand's evil emporium was no more. It was finished, finito, kaputt. It would close its golden doors for the last time that very day and would never again go poking around in the heads of the nation's children.

But Frankie and his friends were not the only ones who had seen the news. In a pink, sugar-cube house on top of a hill, a snowy-haired old lady was simply bouncing off the walls with rage. 'Get me Dr Calus Gore, right this minute!' she screeched down her pink plastic phone. 'The children are out of control! It's as if they have minds of their own!'

But Dr Gore was nowhere to be found. Marvella could rant and rave till the sun fell out of the sky but nothing would change the children's minds. They'd had enough. They didn't want any more. They had had all they could take of Marvella Brand and her sinister playthings, and that was the end of that.

As she watched her evil emporium fall to pieces, Marvella's smile began to crack like an ancient glacier. Then, all of a sudden, as if somebody had pushed a detonator, she exploded into the most colossal tantrum. She stamped and howled and snapped her magic wand in two. She kicked and yelled and beat her fists on the carpet. And she was still bawling and hollering like an oversize toddler when, at four o'clock that afternoon, a cream-coloured envelope dropped through her letterbox.

CHAPTER THIRTY
THE STAR

Eddie spread the *Cramley Chronicle* on the breakfast table for everyone to see. The front cover showed a huge colour photograph of Frankie, Neet, Wes and Timmy.

'Cooooo!' said Neet, as she spotted the headline: *YOUNG HEROES STOP MARVELLA MADNESS*. 'Do you see that? We're heroes!'

Frankie smiled with pride and turned the page. The whole newspaper was devoted to their story. *TERROR IN TOY TOWN* blared another headline next to a picture of a giant Mechanimal swivelling its robotic eyes. *WHERE'S CALUS GORE?* demanded another above the holiday snap of Dr Gore wearing his duck-shaped rubber ring. Frankie chuckled with glee and turned to the back page.

On the reverse cover was a large picture of Marvella Brand standing outside a police car and speaking to a scrum of reporters. Frankie narrowed his eyes as he studied the picture. There was something odd about it. Something about Marvella had changed.

'She's not smiling,' said Neet. And indeed she wasn't. Marvella's famous smile had gone, melted away. Frankie thought she looked like an old snowman slumped in the sun. But it wasn't just her smile that had changed. Her eyes also looked different. Frankie couldn't be sure but he thought he could see the traces of the little girl he had seen in the photograph, sitting on her uncle's knee. Only much, much older and much, much sadder.

'Listen to this,' said Wes, who had been reading the article. '*Marvella Brand's Happyland will close immediately*,' he read aloud. '*But in its place, Miss Brand will open a workshop in memory of her uncle, the legendary toymaker, Mr Crispin Whittle.*'

Eddie raised his bristly eyebrows. 'Really?' he asked.

'That's what it says here,' Wes replied, 'and that's not all, listen: *Before starting her stint in jail, Miss Brand insisted that her workshop would be open to everyone. "All children shall be included," she said. "No child shall be left out."*'

'Well knock me down with a dandelion!' said Alphonsine, reading over Frankie's shoulder. 'And tickle me with a feather.'

Frankie looked back at the picture. He noticed

that Marvella was clutching something in her dry, old hands. But it was not a fairy wand. It was a smooth, cream-coloured envelope.

'What was in her uncle's letter, Eddie?' asked Frankie.

Eddie smiled and buttered his toast. 'I have no idea,' he said, taking a bite. 'I never read other people's mail.'

After such a turbulent term, Frankie just wanted life to get back to normal. He wanted to watch cartoons, go to football practice, and make his volcano model for Geography class. But getting back to normal wasn't all that easy. Whether he liked it or not, Frankie Blewitt was now an international superstar. Every day, the poor old postman would struggle up the driveway with a sack full of mail, and Frankie would spend at least an hour sifting through admiring letters, postcards and party invitations from children all round the world. One day Frankie shook his head in astonishment as he opened a smart-looking envelope and pulled out a stiff white card. It was an invitation from the royal princes asking Frankie to come and spend Christmas in one of their castles. He could hardly believe it. Just weeks before, he had spent his lunchbreaks alone on his bench and now even royalty wanted to be friends. Frankie chuckled to himself and slipped the invitation back in the envelope. All the attention was nice for a while, but he knew who his friends were, and that's who he wanted to spend Christmas with.

And what a Christmas it was turning out to be! On Christmas Eve there was a surprise fall of snow. Frankie and Wes gasped as they looked out of the frosty window at a smooth white landscape sparkling beneath the bluest of blue skies. The

scene reminded Frankie of one of those nature programmes about life in the Arctic Circle and, all of a sudden, a shiver ran down his spine. Somewhere out there, bobbing about on an iceberg with only killer whales for company was his arch-enemy, Dr Calus Gore.

'Are you thinking . . . ?' said Wes with a tremor in his voice.

Frankie took a deep breath, then smiled. 'Well, I hope he remembered his mittens!' he said. The two boys laughed till their sides ached then, grabbing their bobble-hats, they ran out into the snow and swept Dr Calus Gore clean out of their minds.

Frankie, Wes, Neet and Timmy spent all day tumbling around in the fresh, dry snow. They made snow-angels, sucked on icicles and raced toboggans that Alphonsine had hammered together that very morning.

‘We should build an igloo!’ said Frankie as they were walking back home for tea.

‘Great idea!’ laughed Neet, knocking the snow from her ears. ‘What do you think, Wes? . . . Wes?’ But Wes had stopped dead in his tracks.

‘What’s wrong?’ asked Frankie. But Wes didn’t answer. He just dropped his toboggan in the snow and raced towards the house at breakneck speed. Frankie and the others exchanged alarmed glances, then sprinted after him. As they approached the house, Frankie noticed a rusty old car parked outside. His heart started pounding with fear – somebody was there.

‘Wes! Wait!’ he yelled.

But Wes had already rushed through the front door.

Seconds later, Frankie burst into the house after him and CRASH!! He ran straight into Eddie, sending a plateful of mince pies spinning through the air.

'Frankie, Frankie! Whatever is the matter?' Eddie exclaimed, as Colette caught the falling pies in her jaws.

'Sorry, Eddie,' Frankie puffed breathlessly, as Neet and Timmy piled into the house behind him. 'Where's Wes? What's happening?'

'Deary me, calm down,' smiled Eddie. 'We have guests, that's all. Now take off your snowy boots and go and say hello.'

As Frankie pulled off his wellies, he heard shouts of excitement coming from the lounge. He ran in to see a man with curly red hair and a woman with spectacles as thick as jam-jars hugging Wesley tightly and lifting him high in the air. Frankie smiled and wiped his brow in relief as he recognised the surprise guests.

'Mum! Dad!' Wes cried in delight.

'We're so sorry, Wesley,' said Mrs Jones.

'What happened?' cried Wes. 'Where did you go? I thought you'd been eaten by a lion, or sat on by an elephant!'

'We got completely lost, didn't we?' said Mrs Jones. 'Completely lost!'

Mr Jones nodded. 'I was holding the map upside-down,' he said sheepishly, 'and then it blew away and got eaten by a baboon.' Frankie could see that Wes's parents weren't quite as clever as their son.

'We just got home but didn't know where you'd gone. It was only when we saw you on the news that we realised what had happened,' said Mrs Jones. 'We're so sorry, Wesley. We'll take you with us next time. You know how to use a compass, don't you, you clever sausage?'

Wes smiled and clung tightly to his parents' legs. Yes, he knew how to use a compass, and he would never let his mum and dad go wandering off without him ever again.

Once the mince pies had been eaten and the carols sung, Frankie's friends all went back to their families for Christmas. Frankie waved goodbye from the doorstep, then closed the door against the snowy winter air. By the time he climbed into bed, he was so tired he thought he might melt into the mattress.

'Night, night, Frankie,' said Alphonsine, tucking him in tightly. 'Happy dreamings. Don't have any nightscares.'

'Oh,' smiled Frankie, turning off the light, 'I think the nightscare is over. Night, night, Alfie, Eddie. Happy Christmas.'

As Frankie lay in bed, he looked out of the window at the clear Christmas sky. The moon was full as a glass of milk and the stars were sparkling like crystals of sugar. Then, just as his eyelids began to droop, he thought he saw one star moving quickly through the night. Frankie rubbed his eyes. The star seemed to be changing colour from white to green to red to gold and he thought, for just a moment, that he heard the distant sounds of sleigh-bells. Was it a shooting star? Was it just the wind shaking the icicles outside his window? Frankie couldn't be sure. But, one thing was for certain, as he dropped off to sleep, Frankie Blewitt felt fuller and happier than the biggest Christmas stocking in the world.